THE AUTHOR

Sheila Watson was born in New Westminster, British Columbia, in 1909. She took her B.A. (1931) and M.A. (1933) from the University of British Columbia, and then taught in elementary and high schools on the B.C. mainland and on Vancouver Island before beginning further graduate studies in English literature at the University of Toronto after the Second World War.

In the early 1950s, Watson lived in Calgary, where she wrote much of her novel *The Double Hook*. In the same decade, she continued her graduate studies, working on Wyndham Lewis under the supervision of Marshall McLuhan.

In 1961 Watson joined the Department of English at the University of Alberta. With colleagues there, she was a founder and editor of *White Pelican*, an avant-garde journal of literature and the visual arts. She retired from teaching in 1975, and moved to Nanaimo, British Columbia.

In 1992 she published *Deep Hollow Creek*, a novel she had written in the late 1930s.

Sheila Watson died in Nanaimo, British Columbia, in 1998.

BY SHEILA WATSON

The Double Hook

Sheila Watson

PENGUIN MODERN CLASSICS EDITION, © 2018

Copyright © 1959 by Sheila Watson

This book was first published by McClelland and Stewart, 1966
First New Canadian Library edition 1989

Library and Archives Canada Cataloguing in Publication Data
is available upon request.

ISBN 978-0-7352-5332-2

Cover illustration by Frank Newfeld, 1959

Printed and bound in the U.S.A.

Penguin Modern Canadian Classics
Penguin Random House Canada Limited,
a Penguin Random House Company

www.penguinrandomhouse.ca

1 2 3 4 5   22 21 20 19 18

Penguin
Random House
Canada

The Double Hook

He doesn't know
you can't catch
the glory on a hook
and hold on to it.
That when you
fish for the glory
you catch the
darkness too.
That if you hook
twice the glory
you hook
twice the fear.

ONE

1

In the folds of the hills

under Coyote's eye

lived

the old lady, mother of William
    of James and of Greta

lived James and Greta
lived William and Ara his wife
lived the Widow Wagner
the Widow's girl Lenchen
the Widow's boy
lived Felix Prosper and Angel
lived Theophil
and Kip

      until one morning in July

G reta was at the stove. Turning hotcakes. Reaching for the coffee beans. Grinding away James's voice.

James was at the top of the stairs. His hand half-raised. His voice in the rafters.

James walking away. The old lady falling. There under the jaw of the roof. In the vault of the bed loft. Into the shadow of death. Pushed by James's will. By James's hand. By James's words: This is my day. You'll not fish today.

2

Still the old lady fished. If the reeds had dried up and the banks folded and crumbled down she would have fished still. If God had come into the valley, come holding out the long finger of salvation, moaning in the darkness, thundering down the gap at the lake head, skimming across the water, drying up the blue signature like blotting-paper, asking where, asking why, defying an answer, she would have thrown her line against the rebuke; she would have caught a piece of mud and looked it over; she would have drawn a line with the barb when the fire of righteousness baked the bottom.

3

Ara saw her fishing along the creek. Fishing shamelessly with bait. Fishing without a glance towards her daughter-in-law, who was hanging washing on the bushes near the rail fence.

I might as well be dead for all of her, Ara said. Passing her own son's house and never offering a fry even today when he's off and gone with the post.

The old lady fished on with a concentrated ferocity as if she were fishing for something she'd never found.

Ara hung William's drawers on a rail. She had covered the bushes with towels.

Then she looked out from under her shag of bangs at the old lady's back.

It's not for fish she fishes, Ara thought. There's only three of them. They can't eat all the fish she'd catch.

William would try to explain, but he couldn't. He only felt, but he always felt he knew. He could give half a dozen reasons for anything. When a woman on his route flagged him down with a coat and asked him to bring back a spool of thread from the town below, he'd explain that thread has a hundred uses. When it comes down to it, he'd say, there's no telling what thread is for. I knew a woman once, he'd say, who used it to sew up her man after he was throwed on a barbed-wire fence.

Ara could hear the cow mumbling dry grass by the bushes. There was no other sound.

The old lady was rounding the bend of the creek. She was throwing her line into a rock pool. She was fishing upstream to the source. That way she'd come to the bones of the hills and the flats between where the herd cows ranged. They'd turn their tails to her and stretch their hides tight. They'd turn their living flesh from her as she'd turned hers from others.

The water was running low in the creek. Except in the pools, it would be hardly up to the ankle. Yet as she watched the old lady, Ara felt death leaking through from the centre of the earth. Death rising to the knee. Death rising to the loin.

She raised her chin to unseat the thought. No such thing could happen. The water was drying away. It lay only in the deep pools.

Ara wasn't sure where water started.

William wouldn't hesitate: It comes gurgling up from inside the hill over beyond the lake. There's water over and it falls down. There's water under and it rushes up. The trouble with water is it never rushes at the right time. The creeks dry up and the grass with them. There are men, he'd say, have seen their whole place fade like a cheap shirt. And there's no way a man can fold it up and bring it in out of the sun. You can save a cabbage plant or a tomato plant with tents of paper if you've got the paper, but there's no human being living can tent a field and pasture.

I've seen cows, he'd say, with lard running off them into the ground. The most unaccountable thing, he'd say, is the way the sun falls. I've seen a great cow, he'd say, throw no more shadow for its calf than a lean rabbit.

Ara looked over the fence. There was no one on the road. It lay white across the burnt grass.

Coyote made the land his pastime. He stretched out his paw. He breathed on the grass. His spittle eyed it with prickly pear.

Ara went into the house. She filled the basin at the pump in the kitchen and cooled her feet in the water.

We've never had a pump in our house all the years we've lived here, she'd heard Greta say. Someday, she'd say, you'll lift the handle and stand waiting till eternity. James brings water in barrels from the spring. The thing about a barrel is you take it where you take it. There's something fixed about a pump, fixed and uncertain.

Ara went to the door. She threw the water from the basin into the dust. She watched the water roll in balls on the ground. Roll and divide and spin.

The old lady had disappeared.

Ara put on a straw hat. She tied it with a bootlace under the chin. She wiped the top of the table with her apron which she threw behind a pile of papers in the corner. She went to the fence and leaned against the rails.

If a man lost the road in the land round William Potter's, he couldn't find his way by keeping to the creek bottom for the creek flowed this way and that at the land's whim. The earth fell away in hills and clefts as if it had been dropped carelessly wrinkled on the bare floor of the world.

Even God's eye could not spy out the men lost here already, Ara thought. He had looked mercifully on the people of Nineveh though they did not know their right hand and their left. But there were not enough people here to attract his attention. The cattle were scrub cattle. The men lay like sift in the cracks of the earth.

Standing against the rails of the fence, she looked out over the yellow grass. The empty road leading from James's gate went on from William's past the streaked hills, past the Wagners', down over the culvert, past Felix Prosper's.

4

Felix saw the old lady. She was fishing in his pool where the water lay brown on the black rocks, where the fish lay still under the fallen log. Fishing far from her own place. Throwing her line into his best pool.

He thought: I'll chase her out.

But he sat, tipped back in his rocking-chair, his belly bulging his bibbed overalls, while the old lady fished, while the thistles thrust his potato plants aside and the potatoes baked in the shallow soil.

When at last he went down to the creek the old lady had gone. And he thought: Someday I'll put a catcher on the fence and catch her for once and all.

Then he fished himself, letting his line fall from an old spool, his hook catch in the leaves. Fished with his chin rolled over the bib of his overalls, while his fiddle lay against his rocker and the potatoes baked in the vertical glory of the July sun.

Fished and came from the creek. Pulled the fish out of his pocket. Slit them from tail to chin. Sloshed them in the hand basin. Dropped them into bacon fat until the edges browned. Cooked them to a curl while the dogs sniffed. Cooked them in peace alone with his dogs.

Angel had gone. She had walked across the yard like a mink trailing her young behind her. She had climbed the high seat of Theophil's wagon. Now she lived with Theophil at the bend of the road near the old quarry.

He lifted the brown edge of the fish and took out the bones. The terrier sat under the shadow of his belly. The hounds stood, dewlaps trembling, their paws shoved over the sill. Felix fed the terrier where it sat. The hounds waited, their lips wet, their eyes quick with longing.

When Felix had finished, he rolled out of his chair and gathered up a pan of scraps from the trestle on which the buckets rest. The hounds backed away from the door, jostling shoulder to shoulder, tail bisecting tail. He gave them the scraps.

If they walked out of his gate like Angel, he would not ask if they had hay to lie on. His own barn was often empty.

He went back to the table and gathered up the bones that lay around his plate. He stood with a fish spine in his hand. Flesh mountainous contemplating. Saint Felix with a death's head meditating.

At last he threw the bones into the stove. The heat from the stove, the heat crept in from the day outside, anointed his face. Blest, he sat down again in the rocker, and the boards creaked and groaned as he fiddled.

The old lady did not come back to disturb his peace. But somewhere below the house a coyote barked, and the hounds raised their heads, gathered their limbs and sprang into the brush. The terrier sat in Felix's shadow, its ear turned to the voice of Felix's fiddle.

But the hounds heard Coyote's song fretting the gap between the red boulders:

> In my mouth is the east wind.
> Those who cling to the rocks I will
> bring down
> I will set my paw on the eagle's nest.

The hounds came back, yellow forms in the yellow sunlight. Creeping round the barn. Flattening themselves to rest. Felix put down his fiddle and slept.

5

The Widow's boy saw the old lady.

The old lady from above is fishing down in our pool, he said, coming into the Widow's kitchen. I'm going down to scare her out.

The Widow's eyes closed.

Dear God, she said, what does she want? So old, so wicked, fishing the fish of others. Slipping her line under our fence before my boy can get the fish on his hook.

The Widow's daughter Lenchen sat behind the table. Her yellow hair pulled straight above her eyes like a ragged cap. Her hands in the pockets of her denim jeans. Her heavy heeled boots beating impatience into the boards of the floor.

At the far end of the table the Widow was straining milk into shallow pans. The boy sat down and rested his elbows on the other end of the table.

Where's she fishing? the girl asked.

Down at the grass pool, the boy said.

It's enough to turn a person mad, the girl said, to have an old woman sneaking up and down the creek day in and day out. I can't stand it any longer. It's just what I was telling Ma. I've got to get away, right away from here. It's time I learned something else, anyway. I've learned all there is to learn here. I know everything there is to know. I know even as much as you and James Potter.

How do you know what James Potter knows? the boy asked.

The Widow went on with her work.

All you'd learn in town, she said, is men. And you'd be lucky if they didn't learn you first. The things they know would be the death of me for you to know. They'd teach you things it isn't easy to forget.

She put the milk-pail down on the floor beside her, but she kept her eyelids folded over her eyes.

It's easier to remember than to forget, she said.

There are things too real for a person to forget, the boy thought. There are things so real that a person has to see them. A person can't keep her eyes glazed over like a dead bird's forever. What will Ma do, the boy thought.

You've got to take me, the girl said to the boy.

Why don't you just go? he said.

You've been out with the men on the beef drive, she said. You know what it's like down there. I've had enough of round this place, but I don't know where to go.

Place is the word, said the boy. I only know a place where men drink beer, he said. A bunch of men and an old parrot.

He got up and went to the window.

I'm going down to put a fence right across the creek, he said, so James Potter's mother can't go up and down here any more.

6

He went out of the kitchen into the sun. Outside the world floated like a mote in a straight shaft of glory. A horse coming round the corner of the barn shone copper against the hewn logs, Kip riding black on its reflected brightness.

The boy raised his hand.

Kip rode his horse forward to a stop. He rested his hands on the pommel of his saddle and shook his feet free of the wooden stirrups to ease his legs.

There's nothing doing round here, said the boy, unless you've come to trade that bag of bones you're riding for another.

Some day, Kip said. Some day.

Where are you going? the boy asked.

On the road, Kip said. Riding. Just riding. Just coming and going. Where's the girl?

I don't know, said the boy.

I got a message for her, Kip said.

She's in the house, the boy said. Give her the message yourself. I'm not having anything to do with that sort of thing, one way or another.

He went over to the barn and picked up a roll of wire. Then he put it down and looked at Kip.

Kip's face was turned towards the house.

What in hell are you doing? said the boy.

Looking, said Kip.

Get out of here, the boy said. Wherever you are there's trouble. If a man is breaking a horse when you come round it hangs itself on the halter, or throws itself, or gets out and back on the range. Take your message back where it came from.

A'right, said Kip. A'right.

He shoved his feet into his stirrups and gathered up his lines.

The girl don't need no telling, he said.

He bent down over the saddle. His face hung close to the boy's.

When a stallion's broke down your fence, he said, there's nothing you can do except put the fence back up again.

He swung his horse around away from the boy, but he kept his face turned over his shoulder.

Wipe off that look, the boy said.

Then he called after Kip: James Potter's mother is fishing in our creek. It's her I'm going to fence out.

7

As Kip moved off, the boy noticed the light again. Caught in the hide of the beast which picked its way along, its eyes on the dust of the road.

He stood thinking of the light he'd known. Of pitch fires lit on the hills. Of leaning out of the black wind into the light of a small flame. Stood thinking how a horse can stand in sunlight and know nothing but the saddle and the sting of sweat on hide and the salt line forming under the saddle's edge. Stood thinking of sweat and heat and the pain of living, the pain of fire in the middle of a haystack. Stood thinking of light burning free on the hills and flashing like the glory against the hides of things.

All along the fence the road had been cut by the wheels of William Potter's truck. Cut to plague the feet of beasts. To plague the very wheels which cut it. The whole road cut when a day's wait would have let the mud bake flat. Cut anyway, William said, by the feet of the beasts themselves, moving singly or in herds, by the old moose, his face above man-level, and the herds moving, moving.

The boy wrestled with the roll of wire, which curled in on itself seeking the bend into which it had been twisted. The sun beat down on him as it beat down on Kip's horse.

I'm afraid, thought the boy, and even the light won't tell me what to do.

He thought of the posts he would have to drive. He wondered: Is it Lenchen I'm afraid of. Or Ma. Or Kip. Is it the old lady fishing in the creek. Or is it seeing light the way I've never noticed before.

He gathered up the wire and went down to the creek. He looked through the stems of the cottonwood trees, but the old lady had gone. The water caught the light and drew it into itself. Dragonflies floated over the surface as if the water had not been stirred since the beginning of time. But the grass by the pool was bent.

I knew it was the old lady, the boy said. Shadows don't bend grass. I know a shadow from an old woman.

Above on the hills
Coyote's voice rose among the rocks:
In my mouth is forgetting
In my darkness is rest.

8

From the kitchen window the Widow looked out to the hills.

Dear God, she said, the country. Nothing but dust. Nothing but old women fishing. What can a person do? Wagner and me were cousins. I came, and what I could I brought. I've things for starting a girl. Things belonging in my family for years. Things laid by. The spoons. The sheets. The bedcover I crocheted with my own hands. The shame. A fat pig of a girl, Almighty Father. Who would want such a girl?

I could tell you, the girl said.

You can tell me nothing, the Widow said. Go. Go. I hear nothing. I see nothing. Men don't ask for what they've already taken.

She went to the bottom of the stairs.

You want to go, she said. Go. Don't keep asking. Go.

9

Lenchen watched her mother walk away. She kept pulling the tongue of her belt until the belt bit into her flesh.

James had not come as he promised. She had not seen him for days. Except from the crest of the hill. She had seen him below at work in the arms of the hills near his own house. Going from house to barn. Sometimes alone. Sometimes with Greta. She could not imagine the life he lived when the door closed behind him.

She remembered him on his knees in the corral. Holding a heifer down. The sweat beading the hairs of his chest where his shirt divided. She smelt smoke, and flesh seared with the branding-iron. She saw him on his knees with a bull calf under him, the gelding knife bright in his hand.

She heard his voice again: This is no place for her. And Heinrich's voice: She's been at it from a kid, like me. You've just not noticed before. She's been round here always, like the rest of us.

She remembered James's face above his plaid shirt, and how she'd slipped down from the fence where she'd been sitting with Kip and had begun roping one of their own calves so that James could see what he'd noticed for the first time.

10

If Lenchen had been looking down from the hill just then, she would have seen James saddling his horse. He was alone.

Greta was in the kitchen talking to Angel Prosper. William had stopped his truck at Theophil's that morning and asked Angel to go up the creek to give Greta a hand.

She's getting played out doing for Ma, he said. She thinks nobody cares. When you go, tell her I stopped and asked.

And on Theophil's doorstep before the work was done he'd paid Angel her day's wages.

Greta was polishing a lamp globe.

I've seen Ma standing with the lamp by the fence, she said. Holding it up in broad daylight. I've seen her standing looking for something even the birds couldn't see. Something hid from every living thing. I've seen her defying. I've seen her take her hat off in the sun at noon, baring her head and asking for the sun to strike her. Holding the lamp and looking where there's nothing to be found. Nothing but dust. No person's got a right to keep looking. To keep looking and blackening lamp globes for others to clean.

Angel sat back on her heels. She had been moving, half squatting, to scrub the floor. The water from her brush made a pool on the boards.

You mean you're not going to let her do it any more, Angel said. One person's got as much right as another. Maybe she don't ask you to clean those globes. There's things people want to see. There's things too, she said as she leant on the brush in the wall shadow below the window light, there's things get lost.

For nothing I'd smash it, Greta said. A person could

stand so much. A person could stand to see her fish if they had to depend on her doing it to eat. But I can tell you we've not eaten fish of hers in this house. Ask anybody what she did with her fish. Ask them. Not me. I don't know anything.

Why didn't you take your own lamp and go looking for something? Angel said. You've never all your life burned anything but a little oil to finish doing in the house.

What are you saying? Greta asked. You don't even know. You don't know a thing. You don't know what a person knows. You don't know what a person feels. You've burned and spilled enough oil to light up the whole country, she said. It's easy enough to see if you make a bonfire and walk around in the light of it.

Angel scrubbed the last boards, and threw the water into the roots of the honeysuckle which grew over the porch.

They need all the water they can get, Angel said.

Then she saw Ara passing by in the road. She saw her loosening the bootlace and taking off her hat to shove back her damp hair. She thought: William Potter got an ugly one. Then she shook the last drop out of the pan and went back into the house.

Do you want me to clean up the stairs? she asked Greta.

No, Greta said. I don't like people looking round. I won't have people walking up and down in my house.

11

Ara hadn't intended to come to her mother-in-law's. She had wanted to get away from the house. From the sound of the cow's breath in the dry grass. From the smell of empty buckets and dust heavy with sage. She had thought of going up the hill into the clump of jack pines to smell the smell of pine needles. She had walked up the hill, stopping now and then to knock off a prickly pear which clung to her sneakers. But when she reached the shoulder, instead of turning away from the valley, she had cut down through the sand and dust and patches of scorched grass to the road which led to her mother-in-law's.

If she had gone up to the old lookout she might have seen something to think about as William saw things when he was coming and going with the post. She might have seen a porcupine rattling over the rock on business which had nothing to do with her; or a grouse rising and knotting itself to a branch, settling fork-angled so that the tree seemed to put out a branch before her eyes.

Roads went from this to that. But the hill led up to the pines and on to the rock rise which flattened out and fell off to nowhere on the other side.

Yet she had cut down from the hill because she had to talk. She had to talk to some living person. She had to tell someone what she felt about the old lady and the water.

It couldn't rise, William would say. Not in summer. Why, the wonder is there's any water at all. I've known the creeks fall so low, he'd say, that the fish were gasping in the shallowness. The day will come, he'd say, when the land will swallow the last drop. The creek'll be dry as a parched mouth. The earth, he'd say, won't have enough spit left to smack its lips.

It couldn't rise, William would say; but she'd felt it rise.

There was no use telling Greta. Greta wouldn't listen. She could hear Greta's voice rattling like the rattle of dry cowhide: All these years we've never had a wipe-up linoleum. But I like boards better. You know when the floor's splintering away. You know when the rats have gnawed it. I don't like a linoleum. It's smooth like ice, but you can't tell when it's been eat away beneath.

She would tell James, Ara thought. He could do what he liked. She'd be free of the thought.

There were more
than sixscore thousand persons
in Nineveh;
but here were only
herself and William
Greta and James
Lenchen
the boy her brother
the Widow
Prosper, Angel and Theophil
the old lady, lost like Jonah perhaps
in the cleft belly of the rock
the water washing over her.

She didn't think of Kip at all until she saw him leaning over the pommel of his saddle talking to James.

12

James was standing by the barn. Kip's hands rested on the pommel. His face was bent down over his horse's neck towards James.

James, William said, there was no accounting for. He had gamebird ways. He was like a gay cock on the outside in his plaid shirt and studded belt. Myself, William said, I never needed more than a razor-strop to hitch up my jeans. Yet inside, he said, there's something's cooked James's fibre. He's more than likely white and dry and crumbling like breast of pheasant.

Ara heard Kip's voice.

She's fishing down to Wagner's, he said. How're you going to go now? The boy Wagner's there too, he said.

James's back was towards her. She saw him take a step forward. Kip pulled himself up and sat loosely against the cantle.

Ara had stopped at the corner of the barn. James's horse, saddled, waited on the lines. Ara saw it there. She felt the weight of nickel plate pulling its head to the earth.

She untied the bootlace again and hat in hand went towards James as if she had just come.

Didn't you hear the gate? she said.

James started round.

Overhead the sky was tight as rawhide. About them the bars of the earth darkened. The flat ribs of the hills.

Beyond James over the slant of the ground Ara saw the path down to the creek. The path worn deep by horses' feet. And higher up on the far side she saw the old lady, the branches wrapped like weeds above her head, dropping her line into the stream.

She saw and motioned with her hand.

Kip's eyes looked steadily before him.

Your old lady's down to Wagners' he said to James.

She's here, Ara said.

James turned on his heel. But when he turned, he saw nothing but the water-hole and the creek and the tangle of branches which grew along it.

Ara went down the path, stepping over the dried hoof-marks down to the creek's edge. She, too, saw nothing now except a dark ripple and the padded imprint of a coyote's foot at the far edge of the moving water.

She looked up the creek. She saw the twisted feet of the cottonwoods shoved naked into the stone bottom where the water moved, and the matted branches of the stunted willow. She saw the shallow water plocking over the roots of the cottonwood, transfiguring bark and stone.

She bent towards the water. Her fingers divided it. A stone breathed in her hand. Then life drained to its centre.

And in a loud voice
Coyote cried:
Kip, my servant Kip.

Startled by the thunder, Ara dropped the stone into the water.

James was staring down the road. The hills were touched with light, but darkness had begun to close in.

She's going to break, James said. There's nothing else for it. You'd better go in, Ara. Greta'll make you welcome until it's over.

He spoke for the first time.

Kip's face was turned to the sky. To the light stampeded together and bawling before the massed darkness. The white bulls of the sky shoulder to shoulder.

He had risen in his stirrups until the leathers were pulled taut. His hand reaching to pull down the glory.

Ara looked up too. For a minute she saw the light. Then only the raw skin of the sky drawn over them like a sack.

Then the rain swung into the mouth of the valley like a web. Strand added to strand. The sky, Ara thought, filled with adder tongues. With lariats. With bull-whips.

She reached the porch before the first lash hit the far side of the house. She looked back at Kip and at James. James had taken shelter in the doorway of the barn. Kip's knees had relaxed. He was sitting in the saddle.

13

Greta and Angel had been drinking tea at the table by the kitchen window. There were two cups on the table and a teapot. But Greta was standing by the stove when the door opened. Standing with her fingers on the lid of the metal water tank so that she looked across the stove at Ara.

The rain drove you in to see us, she said. Sit down. Make yourself at home.

Angel said nothing. She sat tracing the grain of the scrubbed table top with her nail.

I was walking across the hill, Ara said, and I dropped in to ask after Ma. I thought I saw her this morning down by our place, but she didn't stop.

The room was dark. Greta made no movement in the corner.

You almost need a lamp, Ara said. Did Ma come in? She's too old to be out in this. It comes on sudden in the summer.

She's not been out, Greta said.

She must be sleeping, Angel said. Not a single board has creaked.

She's been sleeping, Greta said.

You've been seeing things, Ara, Greta said. Like everyone else round here. You've been looking into other people's affairs. Noticing this. Remarking that. Seeing too much. Hearing too much.

Who's had the trouble of her? Greta asked. Who's cooked and care for her? I'm not complaining. It's my place here, and I know my place. If I'd married a man and gone off, there's no telling what might have happened. He might be riding round the country in a truck. Stopping and talking to women in the road. He might be leaning over the counter buying thread for somebody. He might be playing the fiddle while the pains was on me. He might be meeting the Widow's girl down in the creek bottom. He might be laying her down in the leaves.

Ara had been looking at Greta.

You've no right to speak that way of the girl, Ara said. You don't know.

You don't know what I know, Greta said.

Angel got up and reached for the lamp.

Leave it down, Greta said. I light the lamps in this house now.

14

The storm which drove Ara into Greta's kitchen woke Felix Prosper. He sat up in his chair. The hounds cowered down, their dewlaps pressed to the earth.

Who's shouting on Kip? Felix asked. What's Kip doing here?

Recalled as if urgently from sleep he looked around for the cause. The heat was still heavy in the air. Felix noticed the darkening of the sky and heard above the beginning of the storm.

Thunder. It meant nothing to him.

Rain. He picked up the fiddle and took it into the house. Then he came back for an armful of wood.

The hounds had slunk off somewhere. Like old women to a feather-bed. He'd seen Angel light a lamp against the storm. Not a wax candle to the Virgin, but the light she'd said her father kept burning against the mist that brought death.

A candle. He had no need for one.

He lit a fire in the stove. He poured water on the grounds in the granite pot. Ground a few fresh beans and added them to the brew. Sat on a backless wooden chair. Splay-legged. His mind floating in content of being. His lips drinking the cup already.

The cup which Angel had put into his hand, her bitter going, he'd left untouched. Left standing. A something set down. No constraint to make him drink. No struggle against the drinking. No let-it-pass. No it-is-done. Simply redeemed. Claiming before death a share of his inheritance.

The cup for which he reached was not the hard ironware lined with the etch of tea and coffee. It was the knobbed glass moulded to the size of his content. Pleasure in the light of it. The knowing how much to drink. How much drunk. The rough knobbed heat of it.

Above him the blow and the answer. The rain pounding the tar-paper roof. The memory of the time Angel had seen the bear at the fish camp. Seen the bear rising on its haunches. Prostrating itself before the unsacked winds. Rising as if to strike. Bowing to the spirits let out of the sack, Angel thought, by the meddler Coyote. The bear advancing. Mowing.

Scraping. Genuflecting. Angel furious with fear beating wildly. Her hunting-knife pounding the old billycan.

He chuckled, remembering the noise and the white face of Angel when he picked up the bear in its devotions. Picked up paper blown off the fish-shack roof.

The remembrance of event and the slash of rain merged. Time annihilated in the concurrence. The present contracted into the sweet hot cup he fondled. Vast fingers circling it.

Then he heard dogs bark somewhere in the direction of the barn, as if they'd found a rat in the manger and raftered it. He looked round for the terrier and wondered at her going. She would not run with the hounds or rub hides for manger berth.

She was equal to a rat her own size. Would tackle one. Like the one he'd poked down. Poked at. For the thing crouching, its tail hanging there above his head, had sprung. Had jumped to the pole seeking it. Had run from pole to arm, its teeth sinking in his neck crevice, its claws clutching mad with dread. He had shaken it off, uncertain in its rage, and her teeth had closed on its throat. White foam on the brown swirl of it. The old lady fishing in the brown water for fish she'd never eat. The old lady year after year.

He heard a bark. And then the soft shuffling thud of unshod horse feet and the clink of bit chains. He heard the step boards creak. He sat, his face pendulous above his horizontal bib, his knees wide, his belly resting between his thighs.

The door opened.

Felix did not move. His bare feet pressed the boards. His hand still held the cup. For a moment he thought it was Angel come out of some storm of her own.

It was the Widow's daughter, Lenchen.

15

The girl stood, the door open behind her. Stood resting on her heels as he'd seen Angel stand when she was heavy with young.

You'd best put your mare in, he said. The stall's empty. You're welcome until it's over.

She turned and went out. Shaking her hair back from her eyes. Walking in her heeled boots as a man might walk. Rolling. Lurching. As if legs had taken shape from the beast clamped between them. Beast turned to muscle twist. Beast answering movement of shank and thigh.

Walked in jerky defiance, Felix thought. Like a colt too quickly broken.

She's been rid on the curb, Felix thought. And felt the prick of steel.

He'd never broken Angel. He'd never tried to. He'd lived with her as he'd lived in his father's cabin. By chance. By necessity. By indifference. He'd thought of nothing but the drift of sunlight, the fin-flick of trout, the mournful brisk music made sweet by repetition.

Angel had borne his children. She'd hoed his potatoes. One day she'd walked out of his gate and Theophil had taken her away in his wagon. Theophil had lived by himself without wife or children. Now Felix lived by himself. Things came. Things went. A colt was dropped in the pasture. A hen's nest was robbed. A vine grew or it was blown down.

He reached for his fiddle and began to play.

The girl came back and sat on the bench beside the stove. The water was dripping from her hair. Her shirt was rumpled and caught to her skin. She said nothing at all.

In the sky above evil had gathered strength. It took body writhing and twisting under the high arch. Lenchen could hear the breath of it in the pause. The swift indrawing. The silence of the contracting muscle. The head drop for the wild plunge and hoof beat of it.

She leant forward a little.

I wanted Angel, she said. But she's not at Theophil's.

16

In Greta's kitchen Angel had set down the lamp.

Ara thought: Why is James so long coming.

I suppose William's gone for the post, Greta said. I'm waiting for the catalogue. There are things one needs from time to time. There are things people think other people have no need of. There are things that other people think people need that no one needs at all.

She turned to Angel.

Take her, she said. I don't want her. I don't want you coming Ara. I don't want anything from William. My post I'll come for myself. James'll come for it. I don't want my things pried over and then brought along here. The government pays William to carry our things as far as your post office. No farther. The government pays you to hand me my things out of the sack. I'll come along and get my catalogue myself. I don't want anyone coming here disturbing James and me. There's been more than I could stand. More than anyone could be held responsible for standing. I've been waiting all my life. A person waits and waits. You've got your own house, Ara. You don't have to see lamps in the night and hear feet walking on the stairs and have people coming in on you when they should be in their beds. I want this house to myself. Every living being has a right to something.

17

James had turned into the barn. Kip had gone off.

He might have climbed down from his horse, James thought, and set himself on the bottom rung of the ladder leading to the loft. Looking wise. Knowing too much. Like the old lady. Like Greta. Like Angel sitting now in the kitchen. Waiting to catch you in the pits and snares of silence. Mist rising from the land and pressing in. Twigs cracking like bone. The loose boulder and the downdrop. The fear of dying somewhere alone, caught against a tree or knocked over in an inch of water.

All around the hollow where he'd taken the girl there was nothing but the stems of trees so close packed that a man had to kick loose of the stirrups and leave his legs flat and push forward on his horse's shoulders to get through them. So still you could hear the frost working in the bark. No other sound except the shift of a horse's hip and the clink of bit on teeth grazing the short grass. But when he'd looked up he'd seen Kip standing in the pines.

He went to the door of the barn and looked out through the rain to the house. Since the fury of the morning he'd not been able to act. He'd thrown fear as a horse balks. Then he'd frozen on the trail. He was afraid. He was afraid what Greta might do.

She had said nothing. She'd not even looked at the door slammed shut. She'd set his breakfast in front of him and had sat herself down in their mother's chair. While, however his mother lay, he knew, her eyes were looking down where the boards had been laid apart.

This is the way they'd lived. Suspended in silence. When they spoke they spoke of hammers and buckles, of water for washing, of rotted posts, of ringbone and distemper.

The whole world's got distemper, he wanted to shout. You and me and the old lady. The ground's rotten with it.

They'd lived waiting. Waiting to come together at the same lake as dogs creep out of the night to the same fire. Moving their lips when they moved them at all as hunters talk smelling the deer. Edged close wiping plates and forks while the old lady sat in her corner. Moved their lips saying: She'll live forever. And when they'd raised their eyes their mother was watching as a deer watches.

Now Greta'd sat in the old lady's chair. Eyes everywhere. In the cottonwoods the eyes of foolhens. Rats' eyes on the barn rafters. Steers herded together. Eyes multiplied. Eyes. Eyes and padded feet. Coyote moving in rank-smelling.

Nothing had changed. The old lady was there in every fold of the country. Seen by Kip. Seen by Ara.

He had to speak. He had to say to Greta: I'm through. I'll take the girl, and we'll go away out of the creek and you can stop here or go to William. Or I'll bring her to wait on you as you waited on Ma. Or I'll bring her and you can do as you like.

He could hear the chair grating back on the boards. He could hear her voice dry in his ear: I've waited to be mistress in my own house. I never expected anything.

He could hear Greta listening at doors. He could see her counting the extra wash. Refusing to eat at table. He felt on his shoulder a weight of clay sheets. He smelt the stench of Coyote's bedhole.

His horse waited, water dripping from its sides. He stood with his foot on the doorframe. Then went out into the yard. Unsaddled the horse. And turned it into the pasture.

18

As James opened the house door the Widow's boy swung into the yard. Water was running from the scoop of his hat brim. His moosehide jacket was heavy with rain.

In the sky above darkness had overlaid light. But the boy knew as well as he knew anything that until the hills fell on him or the ground sucked him in the light would come again. He had tried to hold darkness to him, but it grew thin and formless and took shape as something else. He could keep his eyes shut after the night, but it would be light he knew. Light would be flaming off the bay mare's coat. Light would be kindling on the fish in the dark pools.

He had met Kip on the road.

You and your messages, he said. The girl's gone. I've come to speak myself at this end of the creek. If there's anything any man wants from us, let him come asking on his own feet at our door.

He untied the knot in his reins and threw his leg over the horn. As he came down his feet slipped in the mud of the dooryard.

He can't have her here, he thought. The old lady's out, but Greta's not been off in months.

James opened the door again. This time to look out.

You'd best put your beast in, he said. The far stall's empty.

The boy walked towards the steps.

I'm not stopping, he said.

You'd best come in, James said, till it blows over.

What I've come about won't blow over, said the boy.

Then you'd best go away with it, James said.

The boy saw the door closing. He jumped the steps and caught at the handle, pulling the door open into the wind.

Behind the metal tank Greta stood fingering the knob. Angel sat at the table. And Ara, in the darkness of the room, her eyes wide under her shaggy bangs.

Ara! The boy laughed.

Ara laughed too.

What's so funny, she said.

By God, Ara, the boy said, when I saw you glaring from under that forelock –

You thought, said Greta, coming round the tank and reaching to pull the kettle over the flame – you thought that James had rounded up the herd. An animal can hide in a herd.

Angel stood. She picked up the teapot.

Let it down, Greta said. In this house if tea's offered –

I'm clearing away, Angel said.

I'm come to tell you, the boy said turning to James.

What won't blow will keep, James said. Set down.

I'm come to tell you, the boy said.

He hesitated. He felt the women about him leaning against his silence.

His voice dropped. He turned to James.

I came to tell you, he said, that your Ma's out in the storm. Before it broke she was down to our place fishing in our pool.

Not at your place, Ara said. Up beyond us. Up the elbow-joint towards the hills. Up to the source.

Greta looked at James. Then she turned to the others.

SHEILA WATSON

I ask you, she said, if knowing Ma was out in this I'd not look for her? Do you think James would stand there letting her come to harm? I told you she didn't go out.

But it's easy enough to find out if Ma's here, Ara said. All we've got to do is call her. All we've got to do is look. I've not been up in your house, Greta. It's not my place to go.

I've not been up myself lately, Greta said. The thing about stairs is that they separate you from things.

If your Ma is still sleeping this late in the day, Angel said, she's sleeping quieter than most living things. There's no living being don't turn and creak the bed a little.

How could we both have seen her? Ara asked. How would we have seen her at both our places? She wasn't fishing downstream. She was fishing up, and I saw her ahead of me and moving on. Greta just doesn't know, she said. Go back down to your own creek, James. I saw her there too. There by the cottonwoods when Kip was telling you –

Oh Kip, said James. It's always Kip, Kip, Kip.

Get out, he said, turning to Angel. Go home. The rain's stopped. Is this the first time it has rained? Is this the first time that no one knows where Ma is? She'll come back. She always comes back.

A person has to go out to come back, Greta said.

She walked across the kitchen and stood by James.

Go home, Ara, she said.

Go home, she said to the boy. Ma's my business and James's business. Who's had the care of her all these years that you bother yourself about her now? What makes you choose today to bother?

It was Ma herself, Ara said.

James moved away from Greta.

She'll be back, James said.

32

He opened the door as if to look out.

Kip was standing on the doorstep, peering into the darkness of the room. Light flowed round him from outside. The sun was shining again low in the sky. The mist rose in wisps from the mud of the dooryard and steamed off the two horses standing there.

If you want to go down to Wagner's now, Kip said, I saw your old lady climb down through the split rock with Coyote, her fishes stiff in her hand.

He smiled.

The boy's here, he said. There's nothing stopping you. I just came to tell you, he said.

Greta looked at James.

I knew what you wanted, she said.

She went to the foot of the stairs and turned to Kip.

You didn't see her, she said. You couldn't. I tell you she's here.

Get out, she said. Go way. This is my house. Now Ma's lying dead in her bed I give the orders here. When a person's dead in a house there should be a little peace.

She pointed to the door. But when the others went out James did not move.

TWO

1

After the storm the Widow's girl did not get up from the bench by Felix Prosper's stove. Felix sat looking at her. Her eyes shut. Her head settling on her shoulder. Her mouth loose with sleep.

He wondered: If a bitch crept in by my stove would I let her fall on the hot iron of it? I've got no words to clear a woman off my bench. No words except: Keep moving, scatter, get-the-hell-out.

His mind sifted ritual phrases. Some half forgotten. You're welcome. Put your horse in. Pull up. *Ave Maria. Benedict fructus ventris. Introibo.*

Introibo. The beginning. The whole thing to live again. Words said over and over here by the stove. His father knowing them by heart. God's servants. The priest's servants. The cup lifting. The bread breaking. *Domine non sum dignus.* Words coming. The last words.

He rolled from his chair. Stood barefoot. His hands raised.

Pax vobiscum, he said.

The girl lifted her head. She licked the saliva from the corner of her mouth.

What the hell, she said.

Go in peace, he said. Turning away his head. Closing his eyes. Folding his hands across his overalls. Waiting for her to go about her business. With Angel. With anyone. Leaving him alone after the storm.

The girl looked at him.

I got no place to go, she said.

He'd had his say. Come to the end of his saying. He put a stick on the fire. There was nothing else he could do.

2

I thought it best to go straight on when Angel told me, William said to Ara. The strange thing, he said, is that you should have been there below stairs with Greta and James. What a person has a right to is his kin. There's enough things half-cocked in life, he said, without scrambling out of it any which way.

What a person would like to have, he said, is the grain brought in and the tools wiped and put away and the ropes coiled and the animals in their stalls.

I didn't intend to be there, Ara said. It just happened. I was sure I'd seen her fishing past the house. Then something led me to go and speak to James.

She wasn't in her bed, William said. She was laying on the floor, her rod broke beside her and the line tangled in the hook.

And Greta below stairs drinking tea with Angel, Ara said. And James with his horse saddled about to go off. A house isn't a range, she said. So big that a man can't keep track of what goes on in all corners.

I know, William said, but a man gets used to things being as they are from day to day. It's always when a man sleeps that his barn burns down to a fistful of ash.

But Greta knew, Ara said.

There's no telling, William said, how a person will act. A man would be hard pressed to know what a person would do. James did nothing, he said. He just let her lie. He wouldn't move to put a hand on her. And Greta, he said, trying to send me off before I'd ever looked. You've no notion, he said to Ara, how curious a person can be.

He unlaced his boots and set them behind the stove. He stood in the centre of the linoleum, tracing the edge of a square with his toe. Pressing his toe up and down in his grey woollen sock.

I've handled lots of dead things, he said. But it didn't seem right to lay a finger on her. She was dry and brittle as a grasshopper, he said. A man does what he can. I've seen men die in winter stowed away in trees until spring thawed the ground soft enough for digging. In summer a man can't wait.

He sat down at the table. Ara opened the oven and took out a plate of food which she set before him. He took a knife and fork out of the tumbler on the table and began to eat.

3

Ara left him. She went to the parlour and opened Greta's catalogue. She heard William shoving aside his plate. Pulling his boots on again. Going out through the back to do his night chores.

She opened the front door. The land was humped against the sky. Noisy and restless in its silence.

She went out into the night.

From the corner of the house she could see William's lantern in the stable. She could see him leading a horse out to water. She could hear the other horses' lips moving in the dry hay. She wished she had some living chore to busy herself with now. She'd locked the chickens away for the night. They would be standing edged together on their poles.

The ground was dry under her foot. She thought she heard hoof-beats in the distance. And as she turned back to the house, an owl passing in the dark called out to her Weep-for-yourself. Weep-for-yourself.

4

The boy sat by the lake edge. Ply on ply, night bound the floating images of things.

They had stood like a crowd of fools outside of James's door. He and Ara and Angel. Since Kip had gone off.

Having come together by accident, Ara said.

Sent by William, answered Angel.

Perhaps because he'd had word, Ara said, that his mother was sick or that some accident had happened. Perhaps, she'd said, brought together by sympathy.

And what sympathy could one have for Greta. Angel'd asked. Since Greta never thought of anyone. Not even herself. Only what had been done to her. An old hen pheasant, Angel said. Never bred. Looking for mischief. Trying to break up other birds' nests.

When they'd gone, the boy had hung around thinking:

I'll pull James out and make him speak. There won't be women to interfere. Wondering what he'd do if James answered his question. Waiting for James to open the door again. When he'd heard William's truck he'd ridden round through the brush to the lake, thinking he'd go back when William had taken himself off. Thinking he'd go back and surprise James at his night chores.

Now he sat silent as an osprey on a snag. Waiting. Because he knew how to wait. Watching only the images which he could shatter with a stone or bend with his hand. He heard a fish break water. He did not stir. He heard a bird's wing cut the air. He heard a mouse turn in the hollow of a log.

Tomorrow, he said. Tomorrow is best for such things.

As he rode past William's he saw a light in the barn and William in the barn forking straw into the stalls. He thought of his own animals. He lifted his horse into a canter.

At last he swung his horse up to his own gate. He loosened the wire. Every one of his gates hung well on the hinge. A man could take pride in his own gates, he thought.

All about him as he rode into the yard he could hear the breathing of his animals. Close to the house waiting.

5

Dear God. The Widow waited too. The country. And the moonlight. And the animals breathing close to the house. The horses in the stable. Pawing. Whinnying. The house cow moaning in the darkness, her udders heavy with milk.

A man came when food was cooked. He came unless he'd been gored by a bull. Or fallen into a slough. Or shot for a deer. A man had to come. The horses waited for him. The

cow. The pigs. A man was servant to his servants until death
tore up the bargain. Until a man lay like Wagner in the big
bed under the starched sheets his body full and heavy in death.

She lit the lamp. She shook the pot of potatoes on the
stove and looked under the cloth that covered them. The
woodbox was almost empty.

Dear God, she cried. Then she stopped short. Afraid that
he might come.

Father of the fatherless. Judge of widows. Death, and
after death the judgment.

She opened the door.

Heinrich, she called. Heinrich.

All round the animals waited. The plate on the table.
The knife. The fork. The kettle boiling on the stove.

Dear God, she said. The country. The wilderness.
Nothing. Nothing but old women waiting.

6

In the cabin by the quarry Kip leant across the table towards
Angel.

These eyes seen plenty, he said.

Behind Angel, Felix's children lay, their faces nuzzled
close in sleep on Theophil's mattress. At one end of the table
Theophil played patience. Long fingers turning up a deuce of
spades with a slipping thud.

It's not always right for the mouth to say what the eyes
see, Theophil said. Sometimes, too, it's better for the eyes to
close.

Sure, Kip said. Sure. But sometimes, he said, when the
eye's open a thing walks right in and sets down.

The best thing to do, Theophil said, is to shoo it out. If you had a back door now, you could just keep it moving on. Back doors do have their points, he said, though they're powerful mean for letting in the draughts.

He looked at Angel.

If I'd been here when William Potter came, he said, you'd not gone off the place. I don't care to get mixed up with others. Moreover and besides, I don't care to have you scrubbing for those strong enough to scrub for themselves.

She got herself a dollar, Kip said.

And what does she need a dollar for? Theophil asked. I bring back all that's needed here.

You best move on, he said to Kip.

What did your eyes see? Angel asked. Just what?

Step, Theophil said. Step.

He put down the part of the deck which he still held and stood up. He shoved the door open and leaned against the frame.

Lively, he said. We don't want to hear nothing. We don't want to see nothing.

A tomcat uncoiled like a flame around the door-jamb. Raising its back against Theophil's trouser leg. Bending its head sideways to his ankle.

Just how can I get out? Kip asked.

By putting one foot in front of the other, Theophil said. By getting that carcass in locomotion.

I don't see no way out, Kip said. All these eyes see is a cat and a man filling up the door space. An old yellow cat and a man.

Angel stood up.

Go along, she said to Kip. Phil's boss here. The thing about a man who knows his own mind is that his mind is plain to others.

Not so plain, Theophil said, having let Kip slide past him at the door, having shut the door behind him. Not so plain that a man's woman doesn't mistake his intent from time to time.

Angel looked away.

I had my own reasons for going, she said, when William Potter came knocking.

A woman has no call for reasons, Theophil said. Not when her man treats her good. I make up the minds here. I don't want trouble.

There's trouble enough, Angel said, without anybody's asking you. A man can't peg himself in so tight that nothing can creep through the cracks. Old Mrs. Potter's dead, she said. Kip seen Coyote carry her away like a rabbit in his mouth. There's no one he hasn't got his eye on.

That Greta, she said. She's just making big. A man full up on beer saying in that beer how big he is. Not knowing that Coyote'll get him just walking round the side of the house to make water.

I don't set no store by Coyote, Theophil said. There's no big Coyote, like you think. There's not just one of him. He's everywhere. The government's got his number too. They've set a bounty on him at fifty cents a brush. I could live well at his expense. On the other hand, I'm best to depend on myself, he said, and not go mixing myself up with the government. If you take money from anyone at anytime, it indebts you to the person handing it out. Let's forget it, he said.

Let's go to bed, Angel said, since you're so anxious on forgetting. A man is either up thinking or in bed forgetting. A man feels strongest in bed, Angel said.

Theophil took off his trousers and shirt. He stood in the

candle-light in his undershirt and long cotton drawers. His arm stretched out to roll Felix's children to one side.

This is a thin mean place, men and cattle alike, he said.

The cat stepped up into the space he had cleared for himself. He took it up in his arms and sat on the edge of the mattress. With one hand he held the cat close to his chest, with the other he stroked the fur between its eyes.

7

Outside the cabin Kip leaned against the closed door. Forced out by Theophil under the white lick of the moon.

All the time, he thought, people go shutting their doors. Tying things up. Fencing them in. Shutting out what they never rightly know.

He thought: Angel can see but Theophil's let fear grow like fur on his eyes.

He stood on the doorstep looking at the moon. Stood roped to the ground by his weight of flesh. Reaching out to the white tongue of moonlight so that he might swing up to the cool mouth. Raising his hand to the white glory for which he thirsted. Then remembering: Coyote got the old lady at last.

He went through the shadows of the trees to find his horse. Untied it. Climbed into the saddle. Swung the horse round with a jerk.

He was alone under the moon in the white shed of the world.

I'll go back to James Potter's, he said.

8

Lenchen was coming down the hill behind James Potter's house. Fear rising. Fear flooding her body as the moonlight flooded the hills. Exposed in the white light like a hawk pulled out and pinned up on a barn door for all to see.

She had fed full by Felix's stove and slept a little. Felt the hardness of the saddle under her head, the press of boards, the thin scratch of the saddle blanket pulled round her. Had bedded down for a while in her own gear. Heard from the next room grunts and deep-bellied breath. Taken comfort in huge indifference. Shoved off the terrier which had come growling and sniffing in the dark.

Then she'd slid away from Felix's stove. Crossed the creek on foot and climbed the hill so that she could circle her mother's. Crossed above William's and seen his late lantern in the feed-lot. Come hoping to surprise James at some last chore.

Now, because she was afraid, she crept down into the brush on the far side of the creek behind the house.

James would come. He would take her into the house. Or he would saddle up and take her to town, where men drank beer when they drove beef out for shipping and the red-headed bartender who kept the parrot would say: Mrs. James Potter. I am surprised. Or he would hide her in the hills and creep out with food and covers that he'd somehow stolen from Greta.

But, indeed, she saw him in his plaid shirt his arms reaching forward saying: Did Kip bring my message? Did Kip tell you I was waiting?

9

As if drawn by the thought, Kip came up the road towards her. Nearly everyone else was in bed.

William pulled the sheet up under his chin. His body filled the length of the bed. He rolled over, kicking the covers loose, gathering them over his shoulders.

It's curious, he thought, how a man lies down in the ground at last.

Ara, he called. What's keeping you? A man doesn't expect to lie waiting for his wife half the night.

He heard her pumping some water in the kitchen.

You're mighty dainty all of a sudden, he said. I can remember the time you'd be calling out for me to come.

Prosper had wakened on his mattress. The girl had gone. Her coming had stirred thoughts which buzzed about waiting to torment him. Yet he sank back into the comfort of his flesh, his eyes creased in sleep.

Angel stirred restlessly under the weight of Theophil's arm. Theophil moved aside. Grinding his teeth a little. Shoving Felix's children to the wall.

Do that Coyote really be prying about? Angel thought. Who says where a woman shall lie but that very woman herself. Who keeps chawing at a man but a man's own self?

The Widow lay stiff on her fat feather pillow. She could hear the boy heavy in sleep.

The girl chose to go. How can God judge, she said.

But she pulled the covers up over her eyes to shut out the moonlight.

10

Kip's mind was on James. James's strength. James's weakness. James's old mother. James and Greta. James and the girl Wagner. The messages he'd taken for James.

He's like his old lady, Kip thought. There's a thing he doesn't know. He doesn't know you can't catch the glory on a hook and hold on to it. That when you fish for the glory you catch the darkness too. That if you hook twice the glory you hook twice the fear. That Coyote plotting to catch the glory for himself is fooled and every day fools others. He doesn't know, Kip thought, how much mischief Coyote can make.

Coyote reaching out reflected glory. Like a fire to warm. Then shoving the brand between a man's teeth right into his belly's pit. Fear making mischief. Laying traps for men. The dog and his servants plaguing the earth. Fear skulking round. Fear walking round in the living shape of the dead. No stone was big enough, no pile of stones, to weigh down fear.

His mind awake floated on the tide of objects about him. Was swirled in a pool. Caught in the fork of a tangle. Diverted from its course. Swept into the main stream. Birds' eyes. The veins of leaves dark in the moonlight. A beetle caught blue on a shelved stone.

Not far from James's gate Kip turned his horse off the road and led it across the creek into the matted willows.

11

So it was not James that the girl saw first but Kip. There was no mistake. The moonlight was clear around her. So clear that she could see every split shake on James Potter's roof.

A man stumbles on things, Kip said. Just walking along in the brush. I go all the way down to your place with some words for you and you're hanging about in the house. Now girls should be in bed. And now I just find you sitting outside in the bushes.

What are you doing here? the girl asked. What words did James send?

How do you know it was James sent words? Kip asked. I didn't say James's words.

The girl said nothing.

Supposing James did send words, Kip said. What do you think he said?

Still the girl did not speak.

I forget, Kip said. A man can't be remembering things all his life.

He turned away and started towards the creek.

Where are you going? the girl asked. Come back.

Kip walked a few more steps away from her. She got up from the ground and followed him.

Tell me, she said, what words he sent. Tell me.

Kip looked around.

You got anything to oil up a man's mind? he asked.

Nothing, she said. Nothing worth having. Nothing that someone else wouldn't take back from you. Girls don't have things to give. I've got nothing of my own.

You gave something to James, he said.

Go away, said the girl. Go away. Then she ran.

12

It seemed to her that it was someone else breaking through the brush. Splashing across the creek. Racing up the hoof-pocked path to the barnyard. Running headlong for the door she'd been watching.

She could hear hands beating wood. Each stroke prolonged joining the first. Clamour filling the night.

Yet Kip had not followed her. There was no one but herself in the emptiness before James's house.

James had forbidden her to come.

The door opened outward.

I have broken my word, Lenchen thought. And she imagined the old lady's eyes and Greta's blazing like lamps in the inmost corners of the room.

What do you want here? It was a woman's voice. Greta's. But the girl heard at the same moment the explosion of a match. Saw flame rise gold from its blue fire. Saw James lifting the lamp so high that the light slanting down over Greta's shoulder reached out towards her.

Yet Greta stood almost full in the doorway like a tangle of wild flowers grown up between them. All green and gold and purple in the lamplight. Fat clinging clumps of purple flowers. Honey-tongued. Bursting from their green stems. Crowding against green leaves. Her face above. Fierce. Sharp. Sudden as a bird's swinging out on the topmost surge.

Lenchen shrank away from the riot of the falling skirt. Shut her eyes against the tumult of branch and leaf. Calling: James. James. As if she saw him at a great distance. While behind her Kip's voice sounded. Loon laugh shivering the night.

James shoved Greta aside. He held the lamp high as he came.

Can a man have no peace? he said.

He took the girl by the arm.

Kip came out of the shadow by the barn.

Why are you hallooing about my house? James asked. In a whole miserable country can a man have no rest?

Not when he's got the weight of his doings on him, Kip said.

You wanted the old woman out of the way, didn't you? Kip asked. You wanted to see the girl, didn't you?

How can a man know what he wants? James said.

The girl didn't move.

Greta had gone back into the house. She sat in her mother's chair, the folds of her housecoat falling between her knees.

Send them away, James, she called out. Drive them off the place.

Oh-ho, Kip said. Just the same old Greta. The same old Greta inside some plants and bushes.

You'd best take us in, he said to James. We can't just keep standing about. Tell her we came to help you.

He lifted his face. Smiling.

That Greta, he thought. Standing there proud like the glory. Fitting herself into a glory the way a man fits himself into a shirt and pants.

James stood uncertain before the door.

Come in, James, Greta said. Come in and shut away the moon.

Did you forget, he asked, I've others with me?

How could I forget? she called out. How could I forget with their noise still in my ears. Yelling and shrieking outside in the night like cats in torment. Can you think that I didn't see with my own eyes what was going on out there in the moonlight. It's Kip should have known better since he knew there was death in the house. It's not as if there weren't plenty of hollows in the hills where he could chase his mares.

Let me go, James, the girl said. Just let me go.

Let's all walk in and set down, Kip said. She's got her rope on the wrong horse.

No. No, the girl said, loosening as she pulled forward James's hold on her wrist.

Who's dead? she asked Greta. Is it your Ma? Is that why you didn't come? she said to James.

Come, Greta said. Come where, you little fool?

The girl turned to James.

Say something, she said. Haven't you anything to say?

I told you not to come here, he said. And you come tonight of all nights.

I had nowhere else to go, the girl said. I thought you might open the door with your own hands. I didn't want anybody to make you open the door, she said. No one but myself. What do you want me to do now? she asked.

James looked at Greta.

She sat there, her face flat above the fierce twist of printed flowers.

Tell Kip to water the stock, she said. No one has done anything. Go with him. What use is the night to me now?

Kip had set the lamp on the table. He took the lantern from the shelf and lit it.

He thought: He's only to loose the force in his own muscles. But a horse stays under the cinch because it's used to it from a colt.

He turned down the wick of the lantern. Waiting.

The door was still open. James turned into his shadow and walked out of the house with Kip at his heels.

13

Greta got up and closed the door. Then she turned and caught the girl by the shoulder.

Keep on looking, she said. And think what you want. I don't care. It's what I am, she said. It's what's driven him out into the creek bottom. Into the brush. Into the hogpen. A woman can stand so much, she said. A man can stand so much. A woman can stand what a man can't stand. To be scorned by others. Pitied. Scrimped. Put upon. Laughed at when no one has come for her, when there's no one to come. She can stand it when she knows she still has the power. When the air's stretched like a rope between her and someone else. It's emptiness that can't be borne. The potholes are filled with rain from time to time. I've seen them stiff with thirst. Ashed white and bitter at the edge. But the rain or the run-off fills them at last. The bitterness licked up. I tell you there was only James. I was never let run loose. I never had two to waste and spill, like Angel Prosper.

She pulled the girl over to the foot of the stairs.

I heard her breath stop, she said. And the cold setting her flesh. Don't believe what James might say. She's not looking still. I heard what we'd been waiting to hear. What James and me had been waiting to hear all these years. There was only James, she said. Only James and me waiting.

What do you want? the girl said. What are you telling me for? What can I do?

She pulled herself free and went to the door. But outside was night. Outside was Kip. Outside was floorless, roofless, wall-less.

Let me stop, she said. I've no place to go.

Greta crossed the room.

Go away, she said. Go away and leave us in peace. Don't ask me. Don't put the blame on me. There's nothing I can do. There's nothing I can say. Go yourself while there's still time.

The girl did not move from the doorway.

He'll kill me too, Greta said. He'll shove me down for standing in his way.

Then they heard James's voice rising in the barn. They heard a cry. They heard Kip's voice: You bastard, James. They heard James's voice. They heard his words: If you were God Almighty, if you'd as many eyes as a spider I'd get them all.

They heard a bucket overturn and animals move in their stalls.

Then they heard James's voice again: Miserable shrew, smell me out if you can.

Now Greta and the girl stood watching in the doorway.

James came out of the barn alone. He came one hand swinging the lantern, the other trailing the rawhide whip he used to break his horses. He came out of the barn and up the rise towards them.

James, Greta said.

He lifted his whip. It reached out towards her, tearing through the flowers of her housecoat, leaving a line on her flesh. Then as the thong unloosed its sweep it coiled with a jerk about Lenchen's knees.

Not long after they heard him ride off through the gate.

14

Ara heard and woke. William had raised himself on his elbow and was looking down on her in the thin morning light.

I'm sure, he said, I heard the beat of a horse's hooves.

It's probably Kip, Ara said. Just looking round.

He'll look once too often, William said. But he lay down and reached out his arm towards her.

Angel heard. Got up. Went to the window. Saw only the dust raised by something which had disappeared. Turning saw Theophil and the children asleep on the mattress.

He'd no right to turn Kip out, she thought. He's gone off perhaps, and now I'll never hear the things he sees.

The Widow heard. It's the boy, she thought, going off again.

But the boy was stirring in the kitchen below. Knocking the stove wood into place with the lifter.

She put her hand over her eyes.

Dear God, she thought. How easy death would be if there was death and nothing more.

Felix Prosper slept. He dreamed that Angel was riding through his gate on a sleek ass. He was pulling the scratchy white surplice over his uncombed head. It was early and the ground was wet with dew.

I mustn't forget, he thought. I mustn't forget.

He saw a coyote standing near the creek. He wanted to follow it into the hills. He felt its rough smell on his tongue.

He turned away from the creek and went to the gate. He could feel the surplice straining at his armpits like a garment which had shrunk in a storm. He reached up his hand.

Dignum et justum est, he said as he helped Angel down.

THREE

1

Heinrich too had heard the beat of hooves. He wrenched a stick of wood into place in the stove. Stood watching the flicker of light on the board ceiling. Stood trying to think that he'd heard nothing. That it was a morning like every other morning he'd known.

He went to the shelf and took down three cups. He put the pan on the stove and cut bacon and bread. He heard his mother moving about. He went to the foot of the stairs.

Can't you smell the bacon? he called.

His mother came down and sat at the table.

He gave her her plate. Seeing as he gave it to her her thin grey hair pulled tight from the crown of her head.

The Widow pushed back her plate.

I'm afraid, she said. What is said is said. I couldn't pick up the shame again, she said.

A man needn't hang himself because he's put his neck through a noose in the dark, Heinrich said. What will you do if I bring the girl back?

Dear God, the Widow said. Dear God.

2

Felix Prosper had wakened after his dream. He sat on the steps in the morning light. The hounds lay away from him, their heads coiled under their paws, their backs cramped against the side of the house. The terrier had crept down under the covers. Felix sat by himself. The edge of the step cut into his flesh. He had brought his fiddle with him, but it lay beside him. His eyes looked out on an empty world. His flesh was heavy on his bone, a cumbersome coat folded and creased and sagging at the seams. His hands dropped empty between his knees.

So one grew old. Haunted by an image of Angel come back filled like a cup with another man's passion. Haunted by the image of a boy Felix come back in sleep asking: Can your joy be bound by a glass rim? Is death a fishbone in your hand?

Felix reached for his fiddle. He set it in the soft fold between chin and shoulder. The hounds stirring coiled tighter against the sound. Then something answered in the bushes by the creek. Felix heard branches pushed aside. He looked up. It was Kip. Coming over the rise. Lifting his face windward like an animal.

His shirt had been torn by the branches. His legs were splashed with creek water. His face was a livid wound.

Felix put down his fiddle and got up from the step. His hand reached for Kip's arm.

What's happened? he said. Where have you been?

Walking down the creek, Kip said. Finding my way by the smell of the water. I wanted a man's girl, he said. I'd seen enough to buy her.

Fool, Felix said. But he took Kip into the house and shaking the terrier out of the blanket sat Kip on the bed. He lit the fire in the stove and made coffee. He heated some water and put it in the hand-basin. Then he looked in at Kip silent on the blanket and putting on his cotton cap he walked bare-foot out into the dust of the road.

3

In the cabin by the quarry Angel was getting breakfast. The children sat on the bench by the stove. They were still dressed in the short cotton shirts which they wore in bed. Rolled over on the mattress Theophil smoked, his arm propping his head.

You'll burn up the bed, Angel said. Then where will you have to lie about on all day long and all night too?

It's my bed, Theophil said.

He shut his eyes and drew his knees closer to his belly. Then he looked up.

You used to listen and learn from me, Theophil said. Now you just tell. Right from the squeak of dawn. Telling. Telling. A man would be hard pressed to wedge a word into the silences you leave.

You said you wanted to take care of us, Angel said. Now you just want attention yourself.

It's the way you work on a man, Theophil said. Wearing him out. Forcing everything. I liked the look of you, he said, when you were out of my reach.

Of course, Angel said. Poor and thin as you are. And having climbed up, she said, you'd spare yourself the trouble of climbing again.

She pressed a hotcake flat with her knife.

You needn't spoil the cakes, he said.

Who would be riding down the road just at daylight? she asked.

How would I know? he said. What's it got to do with you? Is there nothing you can't let alone?

It might have been Kip, she said. And then again not. It might have been one of the Potters. There's trouble already at James Potter's, she said, and there'll be more. That Greta's got a whole case of dynamite under her skirt.

More like that James has a stick in his britches, Theophil said.

Angel turned around from the stove. She wiped her hand on her skirt. Then she spat on her finger and held it up as if she were trying to find the direction of the wind.

Oh-ho, she said.

Theophil got up from the mattress.

Get those cakes on the table, he said. Or I'll oh-ho and ho-oh you till you think twice next time before you make fun of me. You came jumping into my bed over Felix's back, and you've got me squatting nice for another jump.

Angel jerked the children off the bench where they sat.

Get into your things, she said. What do you think will happen to you if you doze around all day with your backsides hanging out?

What do you think will happen to them anyway? Theophil said. They'll be stupid and ugly as the rest. They're nice enough kids, too, he said. But I sure don't need you and your kids round here showing me how miserable a person can be. I don't need you or anyone else painting in big letters what's easy to see.

4

In Ara's kitchen William laid down his knife and fork and put his coffee-cup in the middle of his plate. Then he put some more sugar in his cup.

I shouldn't have come away, he said. But a man has his own things to see to. I took it they could straighten things out between themselves. There's things even a man's own brother has to pass by.

Ara sat fraying threads from the edge of the oil-cloth.

There are things, she said, that can't be straightened out. They have to be pulled and wrenched and torn. And maybe just stay muddled up. Or pushed out of sight and left where they are. You can't tidy up people the way you can tidy up a room, she said. They're too narrow or too big. And even rooms, she said, don't take long to get untidy again.

I don't complain, he said. Though for myself I like to keep my gear in order.

You never complain at all, she said. Sometimes I wish you would. There's a sort of dryness settled on us like dust. You're seeing things all the time, but you never look at anything here. Sometimes when your mother was going up and down the creek I wanted to call out: What are you looking at? She was the one who noticed. If we had a child, she said, you'd care enough to complain. Your mother hated me and you pity me. Where can a woman lift herself on two such ropes. One pulling her down. The other simply holding her suspended.

I don't know, William said.

That's the first time I've heard you say you didn't know and really mean it, Ara said.

She pressed her hands against her eyes.

William got up and went round the table. He put his hand on her shoulder.

Don't, Ara, he said.

Don't what? she asked.

Don't squeeze at your eyes like that, he said. I've known men blinded by less. Over a period of time, he said.

Could I be blinder than I am? she asked. Seeing things only in flashes.

He put his hand on her shoulder again.

Why are you so set on scorning yourself? he said. Put on your things, he said, and come up to James's with me. I'm going as soon as I finish here.

He sat down and began to pull on his boots.

If you come thinking Greta's going to light out at you, he said, she probably will. People keep thinking thoughts into other people's heads. I've seen a woman thinking how a man despised her, and keep thinking it till a man knocked her down. It's best to be trusting and loving, he said.

What's loving? she asked. Loving just makes trouble. Look at the girl Wagner, she said. She's got through loving what loving never gave me, and it's as much or more shame to her. I told Greta not to speak that way, but I knew. Was Greta right, too, about your leaning over counters when you're not here. Are you looking for someone else to get children for you? Who is the father of the Wagner girl's child? Tell me, she said. William, tell me.

What do you want me to tell you? he asked.

Nothing, she said. Nothing at all.

I don't know what's the matter with you, Ara, he said. You've never talked like this before. It doesn't make sense in your mouth somehow.

Ever since I was in Greta's kitchen during the storm, she said, I've been trying to fit the pieces into a pattern.

Some of the pieces aren't so far to look for as you think, he said.

Do you know, Ara, he said, for a man who sees so much I've not seen what was growing up in my own yard. It's like a man who stands on a rock looking over a valley. He doesn't notice the rock, he said. He just stands on it.

He got up, but he did not move away.

Suppose the rock should suddenly begin to move, he said. Or started clutching at you like gumbo.

There's too much supposing, Ara said. Yet how can a man escape it since he can't hold and shape the world. I often envy the horses, she said, standing tail to head and head to rump flicking off each other's flies.

And biting one another from time to time, William said. And letting go with their heels. Beasts aren't much different from me, he said, though they've often less freedom. Take my horse, he said.

He could break out, Ara said. He's the strength to defy you. You or any man at all.

He could, William said, but what would he gain by it. He wouldn't know where to go or what to do after the break. I've seen horses, he said, untie themselves and go walking out of barns. I've seen them knock down fences and kick themselves out of corrals. But I've seen them come wandering back to the barn and the hay. Some, he said, are pure outlaw. But there's the torment of loneliness and the will of snow and heat they can't escape, and the likelihood that some stranger will put a rope on them at last.

Or perhaps even the man that branded them, Ara said. There are some men I suppose who follow, their ropes coiled and waiting. Sometimes I think of God like that, she said. The glory of his face shaded by his hat. Not coaxing with pans of oats, but coming after you with a whip until you stand and face him in the end.

I don't know about God, William said. Your god sounds only a step from the Indian's Coyote. Though that one would jump on a man when his back was turned. I've never seen God, he said, but if I did I don't think I'd be very much surprised.

I don't suppose you would, Ara said. Then she picked up the dishes and put them in the pan.

You're right, she said. Let's get ready to go. I've a feeling that perhaps we're wanted.

You might have baked something, William said. But it's too late to be thinking of that now.

5

Before Ara and William had shut the door of their house behind them, Felix Prosper arrived at Theophil's.

Angel had cleared the dishes away and sent the children out, but Theophil had gone back to the mattress. He lay loose there like a dog on a rumpled sack. His eyes sagging half shut. His face twitching and jerking as if in near sleep he sniffed again the rank scent of other men on the grass which grew tufted at his own doorstep.

You're just thinking up trouble, Angel said, the way a man thinks up reasons for what he's got his mind harnessed to do.

Go on, Theophil said, opening his eyes. Go on as if you were reading out of a newspaper what's in my mind. Go on as if my head was as plain to see into as an old shack with the curtains off. Last night you knew what my intentions were, he said, but you didn't know why I intended. Why that Kip is nothing but a go-between for James and his women.

What women? Angel asked.

Well, the Wagner girl for one, Theophil said.

And for two? Angel asked.

A knocking at the door answered her.

Just a minute, Theophil said. He got up from the mattress and pulled on his trousers.

To think, he said, that someone would come so close and I'd not hear.

Well, said Angel, am I to answer or are you set on combing and scrubbing yourself first? What's good enough to lay round in is good enough to open the door in.

But the door opened itself. Was opened by Prosper who stood hearing the words before and after the knock. Who stood listening when the occasion for listening had come and gone. Who stood feeling the sweat leak from under the grip of his cotton cap. Stood feeling the dust nagging the soles of his feet.

Felix heavy on the doorstep. Angel spun round like a flame on the wide boards of the floor. Behind Theophil rolling up the sleeves of his shirt.

What could he say, Felix thought. All the way up the road he'd been trying to form the words.

Peace be with you, he said.

Angel took a step forward.

Forgive us our trespasses, Felix said.

Theophil shoved Angel aside and started for the door.

And lead us not into temptation, Theophil said. His fingers curled into the palms of his hands. The priest taught me the same way he taught you, he said. He spat on the floor.

And uncurling one hand he wiped it across the back of his mouth.

Felix shut his eyes. He could feel the sweat trickling down the furrows of his cheeks.

Angel, he said, I need you.

She drew back behind Theophil.

I've heard those words before, she said. What's the use of going from worse back to bad?

Felix felt the scratch. He put out his hand. He saw her for a moment as a small cat, trying to step her way through the puddles of the world. Fighting the dogs. Mousing for her young.

Angel, he called as he called the terrier. Angel.

Stop bellowing like a sick cow, Theophil said. And get moving. We don't want any trouble here. I don't want to answer in justice for knocking you down. Besides, he said, I'd have to hire a block and tackle to get you off my doorstep.

You couldn't knock him down, Angel said. He could snap you open the way a man knocks open a box. He could split you down the core the way a man splits open an apple.

What's the matter? she said to Felix. I never in my life heard you call on anyone.

It's Kip, he said.

Angel shoved past Theophil and beat her hands against Felix's bib.

What's the matter? she cried. Don't stand there like a lump of meat. What's happened?

He's been beat up, Felix said, and I think blinded.

I knew, Angel moaned. I knew no good was in the wind. Blinded? she asked. For sure? Blinded, she said. Who'll see anything worth seeing now?

She went to the door and called the children.

Theophil sat down on the mattress and lit a cigarette.

Some men get what's coming to them, he said. He stretched his legs out and leaned back on his arm, his cigarette between his teeth.

When she goes off with you, he said to Felix, I want you to know that I've already given her notice. It's the kids I feel sorry for, he said.

6

Go out and bring back Lenchen, the Widow said to the boy. Then together we will think what to do.

Yet even as he began to eat, rubbing his bread in the bacon fat, she began again. Looking out the window at the land fenced off. At the dry parcel which marriage with Wagner had given her.

I had things ready. Things from my family.

Then she stopped. Hearing her own voice in the boy's silence. Her face stirring like ground cracked above a growing shoot.

Heinrich, she said. Then she stopped.

Flesh calls for flesh, she thought. She had paid enough. Had come with Wagner. Her lips closed. Her eyes shut. Had come into the wilderness. She had done wrong. She had seen the wrong. It was God who would judge.

She covered her eyes with her hand.

She had cried out against God. She had set wrong on wrong. She had been judged. Eyes looking from the creek bottom. From the body of another old woman. Knowledge. Silence. Shame.

Heinrich, she said. Go. Go.

Heinrich pushed back from the table.

I've been thinking, he said. In the night.

Ya, she said. You slept. Heavy like a stone in the house.

I should have been able to tell Lenchen something, he said. I should have been able to tell her what to do.

How would you know? his mother asked. You've not loved.

No, he said. But he thought of light blazed into a branch of fire. How could he say that the earth scorched his foot. That he must become ash and be born into a light which burned but did not destroy.

Without speaking he buckled on his chaps.

7

Just after Heinrich passed the lake he overtook Ara and William. They were riding slowly. Ara clamped stiff as a clothes-peg on the back of William's bald-faced mare.

The boy looked at the restless movement of Ara's hat. It had fallen suspended on its bootlace to her shoulders, and slapped and jerked with every forward step of the horse.

Lenchen was part of any animal she rode. Moved with its movement as if she and the horse breathed with the same lungs. Rode easy as foam on its circling blood. She was part of the horse. Its crest and the edge of its fire.

Ara was something else. Made to walk on roads and to climb cliffs. Made to beat her hands against rock faces and to set her foot on sliding shale.

The boy wanted to call out to William: Set her down. You might as well ask a dog to ride with you. But William would answer: I knew a dog once that could ride a horse as well as a man. When the going got rough, he'd say, that dog would move his backside against the cantle the way a man settles his rump.

They must be going to James's place, the boy thought, and moved his hand to rein in his horse. But William turned half in the saddle and called to him.

I was going to see James, the boy said, riding up. But if you have business with him I'd best leave it to another time.

You said your business wouldn't keep, Ara said, remembering the passage between James and the boy. Could a woman ask, she said, what is between you and James now?

William looked across at her and then to the boy who had ridden abreast of them on her side.

It's a dangerous thing, he said, to ask about business between men. I'd thought you might have learned that. The boy here would hardly tell you so much. It would seem like setting someone older and wiser right.

The boy turned on him.

If I can't tell her, who can I tell? She might make things straight somehow. Can a man speak to no one because he's a man? Who says so? Those who want to be sheltered by his silence. I've held my tongue, he said, when I should have used my voice like an axe to cut down the wall between us.

He tightened his legs on his horse so that it sprang forward.

What's your hurry? William called after him.

The boy pulled in his horse and waited.

Why are you going to James's? the boy asked.

What would be more natural? William said. James and Greta are in trouble, he said. And it's my trouble too. Though when a man moves away, he said, he sets up for himself and begins what you might call a new herd. He's not bound to the old one like those who stay. If you moved away now, he said, you'd know what I mean.

But I couldn't, the boy said.

And James couldn't, Ara said. Though Greta might have. And now that Ma's dead James still couldn't unless Greta came to stay with us, and that she'd never do.

The boy looked away.

Ara, he said, you must know what my business with James is. Everyone in the creek must know and no one has turned a hand to help. I don't know what to do.

You have your own Ma, she said.

The boy was silent.

You best wait to speak to James, William said. And you'd best make sure of the facts before you speak. The rest is woman's business.

They had reached the line fence now. The house was still hidden by the sweep of the land.

Lenchen's gone from him, the boy said.

Time and time again I've seen it happen, William said. There's never just one wasp in a wasp's nest.

There's no smoke coming from the chimney, he said to Ara as they rounded the bend. She looked. The road reached before them to the gate, which hung open on its hinges.

William leant down from his saddle and looked at the marks in the dust. Ara smelt the scent of the honeysuckle. But the boy saw a head at the window half screened by the vine.

There's someone there, he said.

William looked up from the dust.

It's Greta, he said, but James must have gone off some- where, leaving the gate open behind him.

Inside the house Greta put her hand on the door bolt as if to feel its strength. She had stepped back from the window when she'd seen the boy's eyes on her.

They're on me now, she said. The pack of them.

What have I done? she asked. What's a moth done that a man strikes it away from the lamp?

There was no one to answer.

Then she heard William's voice: They interfere with a man's proper business. Some eat cloth that's needed for human flesh.

She heard Angel's voice: What do you know about moths? You never felt the flame scorch your wings. You never felt nothing.

She began to laugh.

How much is nothing? she thought.

She felt the weight of it in her hands. She turned to Angel's voice.

You don't know, she said.

She heard Ara's voice speaking on the other side of the door: Greta, we've come to help.

Then she heard William's voice, outside now near Ara's: Let us in and tell us where James has gone. There's nothing so bad that a few rivets won't set it in use again.

She felt hands on the knob. She felt hands twisting her ribs. Plucking the flowers on her housecoat and bruising them. Stripping off the leaves until her branch lay naked as a bone on the dusty floor.

She heard Ara's voice again and the boy Wagner's: Ask her if she knows anything about Lenchen.

There's a good girl, Greta, William said. We want to do what we can. Steady on and open the door.

Then she heard voices again, but not what they said. Then the squeak of a boot as someone walked away from the house. Through a crack in one of the door planks she saw the circle of Ara's hat. Ara sat down like a watchdog on the step.

Greta turned away from the door. She pulled off her housecoat. She rolled it into a ball and stuffed it into the stove. Then she went naked except for her shoes into the pantry and came back with a tin of kerosene.

Ara must have got up from the steps. Greta heard fingers on the door. She heard Ara's voice: Where's James, Greta? Tell me what you know about Lenchen and James. The girl's gone too. We must all help. We want to help you. That's why we came. Open the door, Greta. The men have gone to the barn.

Greta reached for the matches. She laid the box on the stove and poured kerosene from the tin. The flowers in the stove-box were breathing out fragrance which filled the whole room. They were raising purple faces and lifting green arms into the air above the stove.

She heard Ara's voice: Tell me what you know about Lenchen.

She wanted to cry abuse through the boards. She wanted to cram the empty space with hate. She wanted her voice to shatter all memory of the girl who had stayed too long, then gone off perhaps to die in the hills. Die suffering so that James would remember the pain of her. Die young so that James would remember the sweetness of her. Die giving so that he'd live in the thought of her.

She picked up the box of matches.

Don't play with those, Greta.

She turned quickly. Her mother was standing on the stairs.

Don't play with those, Greta, she said. They're hard to get. A person has to know how to play with fire.

Greta. Greta: it was Ara's voice.

Greta lit a match and dropped it into the stove. The flowers raised gold filaments anthered with flame. Greta reached for the tin and emptied it into the fire.

And Coyote cried in the hills:
I've taken her where she stood
my left hand is on her head
my right hand embraces her.

9

At the other end of the valley Prosper and Angel reached the gate. Angel did not come riding a sleek ass. She walked beside Prosper on her two feet, her children tagging behind her.

She did not come in peace. Her voice lapped and fretted against Felix's silence.

Why was it Kip came to you? she asked. Just why?

Now we've come, she said, we've come to stay. There's nowhere else now.

And what's for them, Angel asked, looking over her shoulder at the children, except rocks and ground and wild beasts to play with – or themselves – in the empty spaces. I've thought sometimes it would be better to take them down below out of the loneliness. But if loneliness is being in one's own skin and flesh, there's only more lonely people there than here.

But how do I know? she asked. How do I know since I've never been there. I could guess, she said. One man is one man and two men or ten men aren't something else. One board is one board. Nailed together they might be a pig-pen or a hen-house. But I never knew men you could nail together like boards.

She had fallen behind Felix. Now she came up to him and beat her hands against the flesh of his shoulder.

Take a man and woman, she said. There's no word to tell that when they get together in bed they're still anything but two people.

The hounds had come to the gate. They stood swinging their tails and grinning foolishly at Angel. But the terrier on the step snapped at her as she passed and crowded close to Felix's ankle.

The house door was shut. Angel put her hand on the knob, but did not open the door. The terrier tugged at the bottom of Felix's overalls and began sniffing its way forward.

Angel turned. Go off, she called to the children. If there's food to be had I'll raise my voice.

The terrier was scratching at the base of the door and pressing its nose against the crack. Angel turned the knob, and the terrier shoved its way in as the door opened.

I suppose there is no food, Angel said. Besides it's Kip who matters. Bellies. Bellies.

From the room came the sound of the terrier's voice. Angry. Affronted.

Stop your noise, Angel said. Then she saw the Widow's daughter standing by the stove.

The girl stared at Angel.

I thought, you'd gone away, she said. I didn't suppose you would come back. Not really. I didn't suppose people ever did.

Then she pressed her back against the wall, shut her eyes and began to sob.

There's no use crying, Angel said. No use at all.

FOUR

1

James had simply saddled his horse and ridden through the gate.

Let the world see me now if it cares, he thought.

The world didn't seem to care. James passed William's house. He passed Theophil's. He passed the Wagners'. Smoke was rising from the Wagners' chimney; otherwise there was no sign of life. James passed Felix Prosper's.

He felt the quirt which he had shoved under his belt pressing into the soft edge of his ribs. He pulled it out and threw it into the scrub.

He crouched down between his horse's ears and pressed it into a full gallop. He wanted only one thing. To get away. To bolt noisily and violently out of the present. To leave the valley. To attach himself to another life which moved at a different rhythm.

The horse slowed to a rocking canter. James smelt the sage and the dust. He saw hill roll into hill.

At last he came to the pole fence of the Indian reservation. The cabins huddled together. Wheels without wagons. Wagons without wheels. Bits of harness. Rags and tatters of clothing strung up like fish greyed over with death. He saw the bone-thin dogs. Waiting. Heard them yelping. Saw them running to drive him off territory they'd been afraid to defend. Snarling. Twisting. Tumbling away from the heels they pursued.

He had covered about half the distance to the town below. Now he came to fenced-off land. Signs of habitation. A flume. A gate. Some horses pastured in a field. Still he had seen no one.

He struck into the highway at last. Here, bordering the road, were the market gardens. Men working among the tomato vines. But he saw only the circle of their hats as they squatted among the plants or bowed down over the shaft of a hoe.

A truck raced towards him. Lace loose. Canvases flapping. Shrouded as it passed in a swirl of dust.

In the town below
lived Paddy, the bartender,
and Paddy's parrot.
Lived Shepherd, the game warden,
Pockett, manager of the General Store,
Bascomb, the bank manager
and Tallifer, his clerk.
Lived ten score other souls.

The road twisted and curled as it dropped to the river. James's horse was dark with sweat. It had been on the road ten hours or more. James leaned forward and ran his fingers down its neck. He felt it tremble under his hand.

Below him on the other side of the river he could see the

town. Houses and sheds set in a waste of sand and sagebrush. A crisscross of streets and alleys leading out to nothing. Leading in to the hotel and the railway station which fronted it.

On the near side of the bridge which crossed over the river into the town he saw a car stopped and drawn in to the bank. Shepherd, the game warden, was asleep at the wheel. Sweat streaking his shirt. Sweat matting the hair on his forehead. James steadied his horse for the bridge.

Over the low railing he could look down to the flowing eddies of grey water. He edged closer to the rail. The horse quivered. Its mouth tightened on the bit. The water moved and stood still. An empty box floating downstream was caught and held suspended beneath him. His eyes searched the river bank and the naked silver bars. And there on a bar at the foot of the pier on which the arch of the bridge rested he saw the dark figure of his mother playing her line out into the full flood.

He pulled the horse up. Then closing his eyes gave it its head. He felt it draw to the centre of the bridge. And heard its feet echoing on the boards until solid earth dulled their beat.

2

The horse took him without any sort of direction to the barn where he had stabled it in the fall when he'd driven in the beef. James climbed down and threw the reins to a man who had been sleeping outside the door.

Rub him down, he said. Don't water or feed him until he's cooled off.

Then he walked away.

The lane which went past the stable led to the main street. James walked quickly. He had decided what he was going to do.

Outside the hotel two men sat on chairs tipped back against the frame wall. James looked through the window of the hotel. The clock on the wall opposite the door showed that it was almost three o'clock. He quickened his step. The door of the bank was still open.

Inside the building the heat was contracted and tense. James went up to the wicket. Through an open door he saw Bascomb, his coat off, sitting vacantly at his desk.

The teller raised his head from the balance-sheets.

I want all my money, James said.

The teller's face seemed to be pressing through the bars at him.

I want all my money, James said.

Pardon, the teller said.

James lifted his hand. Then he let it drop heavily on the sill of the wicket.

Bascomb came out of his office. He waved the teller aside.

I'll see to Mr. Potter's business, he said.

I want all my money, James said.

Bascomb seemed to be grinning at him.

Did you say you wanted to close your account? he asked.

Could I say it plainer? James said.

Come into the office and sit down, Bascomb said.

I don't need to sit down, James said. I can do my business standing.

Bascomb fidgeted with the files. The teller had disappeared. James heard him bolting the door.

Tell him, James said to Bascomb, to open that door. I won't be locked in.

Of course, Bascomb said.

Don't lock up yet, Tallifer, he called out. We'll all suffocate.

He had James's card in his hand. James reached for it.

It's curious, he said, how little a man adds up to.

It takes time, Bascomb said. You haven't any cheques out, I suppose, he said.

I don't ever write cheques, James said.

You'll leave a few cents in to keep your account open, Bascomb said. It's more convenient.

It's more convenient for me to take everything, James said.

Bascomb made out a slip and handed it to him.

How will you take it? Bascomb asked.

In tens, James said. It's easier to keep track of like that.

Bascomb counted the money across the counter: ten, twenty, thirty. James watched the flutter of each bill as it fell from Bascomb's hand.

Well, there's your hundred, said Bascomb. He dropped a five dollar bill on the pile. A hundred and five. His hand reached into the cash drawer. Ten, twenty, thirty, he said as he counted the dimes.

Tallifer opened the door for James and shut it behind him.

3

Outside the bank the air was less oppressive. James shoved the money Bascomb had given him into his shirt pocket and buttoned the flap. He would go to the hotel and get a room.

As he passed the General Store, Pockett hailed him.

I've got business, James said.

There's no business won't wait, Pockett said, except cash business, and a man doesn't see much of that.

James went in. There were a couple of men inside the store already. They weren't doing business. Just sitting on boxes in the shadow cast by chaps and saddles hung against the window for display.

I might as well pick up a few things I need now I'm here, James said. A wallet, he said, for instance.

One of the men laughed. Imagine a man wanting a wallet, he said.

James was looking at the billfolds which Pockett had tossed out onto the counter. He bent his elbows on the rough surface and raised his shoulders.

I'll take that one, he said, laying his finger on a yellow-grained folder. It's proper gear for a man filthy rich, leastwise by some men's reckoning.

I suppose you want it put down, Pockett said.

I'll pay for it, James said, since you seem so anxious on cash business. Besides, when a thing's paid for in money, you've got ownership rights on it and can smash it up if you so choose. I'm beginning to see that a man's always best to deal in cash.

Pockett made a note on the back of a bag. He edged his face across the counter to James.

Anything else you need? he said.

So happens I do, James said. You can hand me down a couple of pairs of socks and one of those green and blue plaid shirts. And one of the small canvas bags with a bar-lock.

Getting out of these parts? asked one of the men.

Pockett looked up. James was standing now with one elbow doubled on the counter, his hand clasping his wrist.

Shut up, Pockett said to the men. Business is business. A joke's a joke. A place for everything and everything in its place.

86

Behind him on the shelves crowded tinned meat and pain killer, scent and rat poison, rivets and cords and nails.

This is not your time for being down, Pockett said to James. I was talking to Bill when he was in on the mail. Everything is running smooth up above, I hope.

He reached for the shirt and socks.

Is it all right if I just put them in the sack? he asked without waiting for an answer to his first question.

Better give the boy a new set of drawers too, one of the men called out. Nothing less sporting than a rip in y'r long johns.

If you can't settle for being civil, Pockett said, you'd best decide on moving off those boxes.

I might as well tell him the truth, James thought. Or as much of the truth as will stop him guessing.

He hunched his shoulders round away from the men.

We've had our troubles since William came down, he said, answering Pockett's first question.

I thought it would be something brought you down now, Pockett said.

Ma, James said.

Sick and brought to hospital? Pockett asked.

No, James said.

Not gone? Pockett asked.

James nodded. Pockett looked across at the men.

There's some people, he said, who's got respect for nothing. Man. Nor beast. Nor God Almighty either. Now a man like me, he said, has got sense enough to know when something's wrong. When I first clapped my eyes on you in the street I said to myself: James Potter and the beef sale not on. There must be trouble above. I said to myself: He looks like a man in trouble. There's trouble writ in the hang of his jeans and the drape of his shirt. Yet there's jokers here who see nothing.

He'd raised his voice. The men on the boxes shifted round and peered out between the legs of the chaps into the dust of the street.

Mrs. Potter, Pockett said, must have been on in years. One of the queer things, he said, leaning across the counter again, is I never had the pleasure of meeting your mother all this time. I guess she never needed anything bad enough to come down.

He was adding up figures on the back of the bag.

That'll be three dollars and four dollars and a dollar and a half and –

He took a catalogue out of the drawer and searched through it.

That size of bag comes at a buck-fifty bar-lock and all. He put down the figure. Which makes ten even.

James unbuttoned the flap of his shirt and pulled out a bill. It was the five Bascomb had given him. He tried again. This time he got a couple of tens. He gave one to Pockett.

Why don't you take out all those bills and put them in the wallet? Pockett asked.

The men at the window shifted round again.

I've got to be moving on, James said. I've got business.

Of course, Pockett said. I'm uncertain in speaking on these things, but you've sure got my black-edge sympathy. When's the funeral for?

James turned away from the counter.

How long, he said, do you think a body would keep in this heat? Up above we do what we can.

It doesn't bear thinking on, Pockett said.

4

Outside in the distance the hills bent to the river. There were no trees at all. Only sagebrush. From the street James could see a single sinuous curve of the river, the shadows of the clouds passing over the water as the shadow of the branches had lain for a moment on Lenchen's throat. The river lay still in the sunlight, its thousand pools and eddies alive beneath its silver skin.

James wanted to go down to the river. To throw himself into its long arms. But along the shore like a night-watch drifted the brown figure he sought to escape.

He asked himself now for the first time what he'd really intended to do when he'd defied his mother at the head of the stairs.

> To gather briars and thorns,
> said Coyote.
> To go down into the holes of the rock
> and into the caves of the earth.
> In my fear is peace.

Yet as James stood looking at the river, his heart cried out against the thought: This bed is too short for a man to stretch himself in. The covering's too narrow for a man to wrap himself in.

5

From Pockett's window eyes watched him through the crotches of the hanging chaps. Along the street in front of him was the hotel. To the right the railway tracks disappeared in a bend of the land. The train would go through in the early morning, some minutes past one o'clock.

James walked down the street towards the hotel. He fingered the pocket of his shirt. He had no idea what a railway ticket would cost. He'd no idea where to buy a ticket to. He knew nothing about the train except that it went to the packing-house, no way of boarding it except through the loading-pens. All he'd done was scum rolled up to the top of a pot by the boiling motion beneath. Now the fire was out.

He heard a voice at his elbow. One of the men who had been sitting in Pockett's store was standing beside him. Friendly now. Had come cat-footing through the dust and stood at James's shoulder.

What you need, boy, he said, is a drink: I'd hate to think that a near stranger had come from above and no one laid a dime on the table to help him through his trouble.

Who said I was in trouble? James asked.

You yourself, the man said. A fellow can't help hearing what's said across a counter. There's no one really wants death. It's trouble whichway you look at it.

He shook his blond head.

My name is Traff, he said.

Well, James said, let's go. It's out of the sun in there. It's away from the dust.

He turned to Traff.

It's what might be called friendly of you, he said.

6

The hotel lobby was empty. The calendar marked the month. The clock the hour. It was quarter to five.

Through the open doors of the lobby and dining-room James could see the Chinese cook slipping about in his black cotton shoes. The cook's apron was untied and hung loosely from a tape which circled his neck. Everything had a hanging and waiting look.

I want to get a bed for myself, James said.

Paddy's probably in the bar, Traff said. It's not always handy being clerk and bartender in one.

When they opened the door into the beer parlour Paddy was leaning across the bar talking to Shepherd and Bascomb. His parrot sat hunched on his shoulder.

It was the parrot who noticed James and Traff first. It raised a foot.

Drinks all round, it said, falling from Paddy's shoulder to the counter and sidling along.

Paddy looked up.

James Potter, he said. What's brought you to town?

The parrot swung itself below the inside edge of the counter and came up with a tin mug in one claw.

Drinks on you, it said.

James opened his pocket and pulled out a bill. Paddy brushed the bill beneath the counter and reached for the glasses. The parrot rattled his cup on the bar.

How many? Paddy asked.

Make it a double all round, James said.

Bascomb got up without speaking and went out.

Well, Traff said, that's what I call friendly. He drew up a chair for James, and sat down opposite Shepherd in Bascomb's seat.

Paddy brought the glasses.

Since there's one less, he said, here's one on you. He took one of the glasses and poured some beer into the parrot's mug.

What brings you down at this time of year? he asked James.

Trouble, said Traff.

I hope nothing's happened to Bill, Paddy said.

No, his old lady, Traff said.

James looked up. The parrot seemed to be watching him over the rim of its mug.

She was old, James said, speaking to the parrot. It was the heat that took her and climbing round in the creek bottom.

What would an old woman be climbing around in the creek bottom for? Traff asked.

Drinks all round, the parrot said.

James shoved the two bills which Paddy had put down towards the parrot. The men hitched their chairs closer.

What was your old lady doing in the creek bottom? Traff asked again.

Fishing, James said.

What for? Traff asked.

What would a person fish for but fish, Shepherd said.

No one rightly knew, James said. He emptied another of the glasses which Paddy had brought from the bar.

I suppose you came in to see about the funeral, Shepherd said.

No, Traff said. She's buried. They had to do it themselves on account of the heat. A person doesn't lie softer for satin and polish, he said.

People don't lie easy in our family, James said. He got up.

You're forgetting your bag, Traff said.

Paddy, he called across, how about fixing this gentleman up with a room.

Paddy took his apron off and threw it across the bar. Just keep an eye out for a minute, he said to Shepherd.

When James turned to follow Paddy, Traff picked up the duffle bag.

Shepherd looked up. How come, he said to Traff, that you're so well acquainted with Potter?

That's not your concern, Traff said. It might as well be me as someone else. Besides, he said, is there any law against a man showing himself friendly in case of need?

He followed James out.

The parrot dropped to the floor and came shuffling over to Shepherd.

Drinks all round, he said, pulling at Shepherd's ankle.

O shut up, Shepherd said.

7

Paddy had gone behind the desk in the lobby. He reached for a key. He handed it to James.

That'll be four dollars, he said.

You giving him the bridal suite? Traff asked.

What's that to you? James said. Mind your own damn business.

I was only trying to save you, Traff said.

James felt in his pocket for a bill. Paddy unlocked the till and counted six dollars out onto the desk.

James thought: I've eight tens, this six and thirty cents. The thirty cents embarrassed him. He took it out and put it down in front of Paddy.

Buy the parrot some beer, he said. It's little enough he must have to live for. One parrot in this whole bloody universe of men.

He doesn't seem to care, Paddy said, picking up the dimes. He gets his way because he's a unique. Men don't often have their own way. It's not many have the rights of a dumb beast and a speaking man at the same time.

James turned from the desk. It was six-thirty. In the dining-room men were sitting over empty dishes, their bodies shoved forward, their elbows resting on the cloth. The room was filled with smoke and silence.

James put the bills Paddy had given him in his pocket.

What you need is some hard liquor, Traff said. But I'm not in a position to stand you to that. I know where I can get it, though. Give me the price of a bottle, and I'll go over while you put your things upstairs. Then we can go round to Felicia's and see the crowd.

Paddy had stopped at the door of the bar and was listening.

Get on about your business, Traff said to him. You can't expect Shepherd to wait forever. He's not paid for doing double duty the way you are.

He took the bill which James gave him and went out.

Paddy walked back across the lobby.

We don't know any good of Traff round here, he said to James.

When I want your advice I'll ask for it, James said.

Paddy turned and went back into the beer parlour. James could hear the parrot's voice raised on a note of authority and the sound of feet bringing men in from outside. He took the seventy-six dollars out of his pocket and put them into his wallet.

He picked up his bag and went to the foot of the stairs. The stairway was quite empty. He looked back over his shoulder across the lobby. The bar door was half open, and through the opening he saw Paddy looking at him.

When I need any man's help, James said, I'll ask for it.

8

The room above was furnished with a bed, a chair, and a dresser. James locked the door behind him. He opened the drawers of the dresser one by one. There was nothing in the drawers except some folded newspaper, a hairpin, and a chamber-pot. James ran his hand over the striped bedcover and peered underneath the bed. He picked up the chair and set it down again. Then he changed his shirt and socks.

When Traff came back after a long time, James opened the door and went out with him.

9

Outside, night seeped up from the ground and down from the sky. Through the strip of purple and green light Traff took James down past the stable to the river flats where the half-breeds had settled, and the Chinamen who owned the market gardens. Felicia's house stood beyond the shacks and out-houses on the clay bank of the river.

Traff opened the door himself.

I've brought a friend, he said.

In one corner of the room, on a bedspring and mattress propped up on blocks, sat a woman. In the lamplight and shadow James could not see whether she was young or old.

Bring him in, the woman said. Any friend of yours is welcome. Anyone's welcome who comes here looking for a little company.

The room was hot. Filled with the odour of bodies and kerosene burning away. Tainted with the damp smell of mud and dead fish.

There was another man in the room and two girls. The girls lay on the end of the bed, their arms linked, their feet shuffling together on the floor. The lamp cast a shadow under the arched hollow between their shoulders and buttocks.

Jimmy brought along a bottle, Traff said. He's in trouble and needs cheering up.

The woman got up from the bed.

Any friend of Traff's is all right, she said. Her body was tight in its cotton dress. She went across the room and took the bottle from Traff.

You fellows eaten? she asked.

No, Traff said. What have you got? How about some picked herrings and onions?

You got the price? the woman asked.

Sure, James said. Bring anything. It's a long time since I ate.

Give us the bottle, Fleeza, one of the girls said, rolling over on her side.

Hands off, Lilly. Traff said. That's man's stuff and old woman's stuff. He reached out and, pulling Felicia towards him, lifted her chin with his fingers.

Everything's fifty-fifty with this one, he said, and a settled account.

It's my business, Felicia said. When pleasure's your business, there's no call to give more than you get.

The two of them went into the kitchen together. The man who had been sitting on a box got up and followed them.

Lilly twisted round towards James.

Sit down, she said.

The other girl turned over on her belly and propped her chin in her hands.

Where did Traff pick you up? she asked.

He didn't pick me up, James said. We just happened together. No obligation on either side.

The girl behind Lilly wriggled closer.

What sort of trouble are you in? she asked. Did you pop someone or something?

Shut up, Christine, Lilly said. If a man's in trouble, he's got enough to think about without people asking.

Traff looked in from the kitchen, his yellow head gleaming in the lamplight.

Don't let them bother you, he said. We'll be out with the food right away.

James knew then why he was drawn to Traff. It was the cap of hair, straight and thick and yellow as Lenchen's. He looked at the two heads beside him. At the dark faces. At the thin and angled bodies.

Traff means all right, Christine said.

We all mean all right, Lilly said. It's just there's no future in it. Drinking and crying, and everything being washed up the next day.

No, James said.

He took out his wallet and put ten dollars on the bed.

They can take it for food, he said. It's little enough to get shut of eating a mess of picked fish.

10

Outside James could hear the flow of the river. The air was cooler. The night pressed against his eyes. He slipped down over the slanted edge of the bank to the sandbar. For the first time in his life he felt quite alone. If his mother was there, he could not feel even a vibration of her shadow in the darkness.

But almost at once he heard the clay slipping behind him and the sound of a stone loosed and in motion. In a moment Lilly stood beside him.

What are you doing? she asked.

I don't know, he said. Looking for something I hope is lost.

Why bother? she asked.

I guess I want to be sure, he said. I can't remember the time I've been sure of anything.

What do you go taking up with Traff for? she said. He's not your kind. If he had money in his purse, he'd not just sit on a bed and go off. Not without taking what he'd paid for. Even when he hasn't any money, she said, there's a lot he takes for granted.

I left the money there for Fleeza, she said.

Why did you come down here after me? James asked.

Because I like you, she said. Because, she said, you just sat there looking miserable when another man would have had his hands already on our skirts.

She came towards him in the darkness. Then he felt her hand on his sleeve.

It's all now with Traff, Lilly said. It's what he wants and quick.

Do you really believe I'm different from Traff, James said.

He shook her hand from his sleeve.

Leave me alone, he said. I've enough harm to answer for.

But he stood where he was, hearing her breath hard in the darkness.

Go away, he said, putting his own hand on her arm.

She turned towards him. Her hands pressed against his chest. Running like fire from his arms to his thighs.

Go away, he said. His arm pulled her close. His face pressed into the angle of her neck.

He felt the fire of her hand and the night lifting above him.

Then she was gone.

He heard her hand on the bushes as she pulled herself up the bank. Her foot on the sliding clay. He heard Traff's voice and the click of a latch. The night was empty about him.

11

He climbed the bank. Through Felicia's window he saw Traff sitting at Felicia's table counting a handful of bills: ten, twenty, thirty, forty, fifty, sixty, two, four, six. Lilly was sitting on the edge of the table resting back on her hands. In one of them she held a wallet. He put his hand up to his pocket. His wallet was gone.

Traff's head shone yellow in the lamplight. James had no desire to move. He watched Traff curiously. Traff put the bills in his pocket. Got up. Took the lid off the stove and, reaching for the wallet, tossed it into the fire-box. James saw him put the lid back. He wondered where Christine, Felicia and the other man were. Traff had gone over to Lilly. As he bent over her she curled her legs behind the bend of his knees. They were both laughing.

Alone outside the glass of the cabin window James laughed too. Laughed looking in at someone else. The price of his escape lay snug in one of Traff's trouser pockets. Traff was bending closer. The girl's hands were on his shoulders. James turned away from the cabin.

The life which Traff and Lilly led behind Felicia's dull glass belonged under Felicia's narrow roof. In the distance across the flats James could see the lights of the station and across from them the lights of the hotel where the parrot who lived between two worlds was probably asleep now, stupid with beer and age.

James stood for a moment in the moonlight among the clumps of stiff sage which shoved through the seams and pockets of the earth.

FIVE

1

Wiiliam stood looking into the charred roots of the one suckle.

What use, he asked, could even three people be since the door was barred and there was nothing but a half-empty bucket among them.

It's the horror, he said, of what you find. Fire doesn't burn clean. The things you see, he said. Beds standing when there's no one left to lie in them, and bits of dishes when there's no one left to eat. But I never expected, he said, to see the bones of my own sister lying in the ashes of our own house. A hammer never hits once, he said. It gets the habit of striking.

The boy turned his streaked face away from the smoke and embers.

Ara was sitting on the ground, her arms holding her knees close to her chest, her eyes on the boy's scorched and torn shirt.

The words of the lord came, saying: Say now to the rebellious house, Know you not what these things mean?

Greta had inherited destruction like a section surveyed and fenced. She had lived no longer than the old lady's shadow left its stain on the ground. She sat in her mother's doom as she sat in her chair.

Greta was the youngest of us all, William said. You wouldn't know how she was. Sliding down the stacks and falling into the creek. Ma was hard on her, he said. She thought grief was what a woman was born to sooner or later, and that men got their share of grief through them. I've no cause myself to complain, he said, but a man hardly lives long enough to prove a point for certain. Mostly too, he said, when he's proved it he's lost the care to know.

The smoke rose from the charred logs. They had stopped the fire from spreading, but they had not stopped the fire.

Prophesy upon these bones, Ara thought. Then she hid her face in her hands. She was afraid she would feel the earth shake and see the bones come together bone to bone. That the wind would blow and she would see Greta fleshed and sinewed standing on the ruin she had made.

We've no more chance of finding your sister, William said to the boy, than we had of putting out the fire. It would be like searching a dog for fleas with a comb that had only a couple of teeth. She might have gone off with James, he said.

The boy turned to him.

So I wasn't wrong, after all, he said. She might have gone off with James. You told me I'd best make sure of the facts. They were probably as clear to you as they were to me. You don't have to spy your way along an actual built fence to know the probable lay of the land.

Ara sat looking at the smoking doorsill. The door of the house had opened into the east wind. Into drought. She remembered how she'd thought of water as a death which might seep through the dry shell of the world. Now her tired eyes saw water issuing from under the burned threshold. Welling up and flowing down to fill the dry creek. Until dry lips drank. Until the trees stood knee deep in water.

Everything shall live where the river comes, she said out loud. And she saw a great multitude of fish, each fish springing arched through the slanting light.

She looked at the man and at the boy.

How can you go on so? she asked.

What does a man do, the boy asked, when there's nothing to be done but dig a grave?

He digs a grave, Ara said, and holds his peace.

Above them a coyote barked. This time they could see it on a jut of rock calling down over the ledge so that the walls of the valley magnified its voice and sent it echoing back:

Happy are the dead
for their eyes see no more.

If we don't move, the boy said, night will be on us, and by the morning there will be no bones to bury.

I've seen the place where a cow stumbled, William said, licked clean before daybreak.

What are we going to do? the boy asked.

We've definite things to think about, William said. First of all James is bound to come back. He's not one to throw himself into a pit, though he might stand on the edge looking in.

Let's do what we have to, the boy said. Ma'll be waiting and my stock and yours.

I'll go, Ara said. I might as well be what use I can. I'll ride down from our place to yours and spend the night with your mother. If James is bound to come back, there'd best be someone here.

2

The Widow Wagner had waited all day. She moved about the house shifting a chair, a dish, a pile of clothing. At last she went to the wooden box which stood at the foot of her bed.

She opened the lid and knelt down. Underneath Wagner's suit, underneath his shoes wrapped in flour sacking, underneath his drawers and shirts, was cloth of her own spinning, cloth left from the time when she had made her own children's clothes.

Dear God, she said, how could I know?

She went back to the chest and took out Wagner's heavy metal watch. She'd meant to give it to the boy. She'd meant a great many things.

What is time, she thought, but two hands shaking us from sleep. Fifty years or twenty. Forty years in the wilderness. What help a bed and a good goose pillow?

Forty years, she said. Then she put the watch back into the box and closed the lid.

She picked up the cloth and went down to the kitchen. She spread the cloth on the table and took the shears out of the drawer. And out of the cloth she cut a baby's singlet.

3

Meanwhile Angel had gone about her work.

There's no use crying, she said to the girl. No use at all.

Water, she said to Felix. Her finger pointed to the buckets on the bench. Then she turned and went into the other room.

Kip, she called. What's the matter, Kip?

It's my eyes, Kip said, but I had it coming. There's no time a bug won't get its wings frayed in the end.

I'd a feeling you'd get into trouble, Angel said. Phil had no right to turn you out. I might just as well have been shut of him soon as late. When suspicion buzzes on a mind like his, the maggots eat right in.

Tell the girl, Kip said, that I didn't mean nothing. The old white moon had me by the hair.

The girl was standing at the door looking in.

You wouldn't know what he said, she muttered.

I can suspect, Angel said. It wouldn't take a great stretch to imagine.

She knelt down by the bed and took Kip's face in her hands.

Who'll see things now, she said. The bugs. The flowers. The bits of striped stone.

The girl was crying again.

It was me, she said. All because of me the whole world's wrecked, she said.

The whole world is a big lot for one girl to wreck, Angel said.

She pulled the blanket round Kip.

Lay still, she said, till I get some water.

She stood up.

Go back into the kitchen, she said to the girl. There's still some ground to walk on, and I figure there isn't a single inch tore out of the sky. When you wreck the world you won't stand round talking about it.

She walked into the kitchen behind the girl.

If I did right, she said, I'd pack you up and send you back to your ma.

The girl sat down on the bench beside the stove.

I'll do what you want, she said. Only let me stop.

She put out her hand towards Angel.

He hit me, she said. James hit me.

And well he might, Angel said, if you were snivelling the way you're snivelling now.

Felix, she called through the door. Felix, are you waiting for the rain to fill your buckets.

Angel, the girl said.

Angel turned. I thought you'd done, she said.

He went away, the girl said. He got on his horse and went off. He just left me there with Greta.

Angel paid no attention.

Felix, she called. Felix.

But Felix was already in the doorway. He held the bail of the bucket askew so that the water slopped over and left a dark stain on the leg of his overalls.

I saw James Potter's old mother standing by my brown pool, he said. I was thinking of catching some fish for the lot of us. But she wasn't fishing, he said. Just standing like a tree with its roots reaching out to water.

Give me the bucket, Angel said. There's things to be done needs ordinary human hands.

4

The Widow sat with the singlet half finished in her lap. She could hear the calf bawling in the yard outside. She got up and put another stick on the stove. The lids of the pots rose and fell.

How long this time? she thought.

She put on her black sweater and took the cloth off the milking-pail. The calf was in the yard. The cow was in the pasture beyond. As she let down the bars, the calf pressed close at her side.

When the last bar fell the calf shoved past her. The cow raised her head. Spoke to the calf. Was licking its neck and flanks.

Wait till I come, the Widow called.

The cow and the calf paid no attention to her.

Shoo, she said, lifting her apron and shaking it. She put down her pail and took hold of the calf's tail. The calf's legs stiffened. It kept its head down. She could see the movement of its throat and the milk dribbling from the corners of its mouth.

Stop, she cried.

But the calf drank on, its tail slipping through her fingers like rope.

Help, help, she called to the cow. We're old women both of us.

The cow adjusted her hip. She raised her horns a little and breathed heavily through her black nostrils.

5

When Ara came she turned the calf back into the yard. She watered the horses and threw hay down to them.

I've wasted the milk, the Widow said. There will be none for the children.

She had set food out for three.

I hate to think of the men, Ara said as she sat down. They haven't a bite between them. There's a sort of shame in eating when grief is everywhere.

She leant over and picked up the shirt which the Widow had left on the chair.

So you do know, she said. It would be hard to believe that you didn't.

The Widow shut her eyes. Dear God, she said, there's nothing one can hide.

Too much has happened, Ara said, to talk of hiding. James's mother's dead. Her house has burned down and Greta in it. Your house is standing and your children are alive.

Lenchen will suffer like the rest of us, the Widow said. She's done wrong.

Right and wrong don't make much difference, Ara said. We don't choose what we will suffer. We can't even see how suffering will come.

She tossed the shirt onto the couch under the window.

I never see baby-clothes, she said, that I don't think how a child puts on suffering with them.

6

In the cabin by the quarry Theophil slept again. His body turned and twitched on the mattress. Outside the yellow cat rubbed against the door, waiting to be let in.

7

Below in Felix's house there was no noise except the stir and breath of living things. Angel had moved Kip from the bed. He lay now on a network of branches which she'd made Felix cut and carry into the house. The scent of pine needles filled the room. Angel sat by the stove. The girl lay curled round in a blanket, her head propped against the saddle Felix had brought from the barn.

Angel got up and went to the bedroom door. In the shadow of the moonlight she could see Felix lying like a rock rooted in the middle of the bed. About him lay his children. And safe in the crevice of his hip the terrier crouched alert and watching with its amber eyes the figure in the doorway.

The girl moaned. Angel turned back to her. She put a stick in the stove and filled the kettle. The girl muttered in her sleep. Angel bent over her. The girl whimpered and moved her knees. She opened her eyes and spoke to Angel.

Will James come? she said.

Kip stirred on his bed of branches.

Tell James I didn't mean any harm, he said. If anyone should ask, I was just riding along and fell into a bed of prickly pear.

Hush, Angel said. Night's for sleep when you have a place to lay your head.

8

James looked back over his shoulder at the moonlight slanting on the roof of Felicia's shack. There where the moonlight slid down the walls Traff and Lilly swam in the pool of silver they had stolen.

The flick of a girl's hand had freed James from freedom. He'd kissed away escape in the mud by the river. He thought now of Lenchen and the child who would wear his face. Alone on the edge of the town where men clung together for protection, he saw clearly for a moment his simple hope.

He had walked away from the cabin. He skirted the main street and went back to the barn. The barn door was locked, and he had to pound on the door to waken the owner who lived in the barn with the horses.

I'll saddle for myself, James said. Then he remembered that he'd nothing left to pay for the horse's hay and stabling.

Write it down, he said. I'll pay when I'm next in town. There are times when a man spends more than he has and must go on credit.

He led the horse out of the barn and swung into the saddle.

Unless a man defaults, he said, a debt is a sort of bond.

The horse turned of its own accord towards the bridge. James gave it its head. It tossed its mane and held the bit lightly between its teeth. Freed from the stable, it turned its head towards home.

James felt the muscles moving under him. Then he heard the hollow ring of hooves on the bridge. The bridge lay a black arch over the clear sweep of the river. And in the shadow of the girders fear unwound itself again like the line from his mother's reel.

Where is your hope?
Better go down to the bars of the pit
Better rest in the dust
Justice is swifter than water.

But the horse carried James across the bridge and up a path onto the shoulders of the hills. The dead grass snapped beneath the horse's feet as it moved, and the dust rose like spray in the moonlight from the sweep of its fetlocks.

James leaned forward. The horse raced from the ridge

through a meadow of wild hay watered by some hidden spring. It slowed to a lope, to a canter, to a pace.

Hills rose again on the other side of the meadow. James could feel the pull of the horse's shoulders as it stepped its way up through the rocks and bushes. He could feel the muscles contract and tighten as the horse began its descent on the other side.

At the bottom they came to a creek. James could hear the horse's feet parting the water. He could hear the flow of water on stones, but in this skyless slit the water was opaque and formless. He shut his eyes and fastened his free hand in his horse's mane.

As they climbed again, the horse seemed to draw life with every breath. It climbed. It rounded ledges. It held close to the rock where nothing but the feel of stone marked the fall below.

9

In Felix's kitchen the girl turned again and groaned. She yelped and sat up.

When's your time? Angel asked.

How would I know, the girl said.

There's not much doubt, Angel said. And the house already crowded to the corners.

She sat back in her chair.

If you were one of mine she said, and I was no further than your ma is from here I'd want to come no matter what I'd said or done. A woman sharpens herself to endure. Since she can be trod on like an egg, she grows herself to stone.

She got up and went to the door of the bedroom.

Felix, she called, get up.

The terrier growled. Felix did not stir. Angel called again. He turned.

I'm going for the Widow, she said.

Felix got out of bed. He still wore his bib overalls.

I couldn't do anything but play the fiddle, he said.

10

Neither Ara nor the Widow could sleep. They had cleared away the dishes and sat talking.

Dear God, the Widow said, she may be alone like some animal in the wood.

James might have planned to meet her, Ara said. He wasn't there. The day his mother died he had his horse saddled and waiting. But he never in all his life had strength enough to set himself against things.

The Widow shook her head.

We can only guess, she said. It's best not to think.

11

It was a knock on the door which disturbed them at last.

Dear Father, said the Widow, throwing her apron over her head, what shall I say? What must I do?

Ara opened the door.

It's Angel, she said.

What does she want? the Widow asked. Speak, woman, speak. Do you know where the child is, God forgive her and me. Dear God, she said, I who wouldn't drive a whelping dog out of the yard have done this.

Angel did not answer.

Can you harness the wagon? she asked Ara.

Then she turned to the Widow.

We've got to get you down to Felix Prosper's somehow, she said. There's no use wailing on God.

No one thought of Felix, Ara said.

12

Felix played the fiddle. The children slept on. Kip raised himself on his elbow to listen.

Light a light, the girl said. I want to see.

It will be daylight soon, Felix said.

The girl could hear his arm rubbing against the cloth of his overalls. She could hear the pad of his foot beating out the rhythm.

What if Angel doesn't come? she asked.

She'll come, Felix said.

Why did she go? the girl said. What good could it do?

She put out her hand and grasped Felix's knee.

Felix, she said, I want Angel. Felix, she cried, I'm afraid. Will it hate to be born? Will it blame me all the years of its life?

Go away, she called out. Let me be.

Felix put down his fiddle. He went to the bedroom door. The light was turning blue at the window. A bird rattled about in the bushes. The hounds rubbed softly at the base of the door.

The girl's voice filled the cabin.

It might be dead, she cried. Nobody wants it. Nobody. It might have a scar like the lash of a whip. Felix, she called, come back. Come back. There's a flower growing against the wall and it's reaching out to cover me.

She's thinking of Greta, Kip said. What did she and James do? he asked the girl.

Nothing, she moaned. Nothing. James is coming I tell you. I can hear his horse's feet snapping the twigs. I can feel the beat of its hooves trembling the ground.

Then she began to cry again.

It's me, she sobbed, outside in the night. Open the door.

Felix shook the children out of bed. The terrier yelped as he pushed it with his hand.

Outside, he said. Get going.

Take something to cover your backsides, Felix bellowed. You can lie with the hounds or in the hay.

He went back to the kitchen and bent over the girl. Her arms were round his neck. He could feel her shaking and biting at his shoulder. He carried her in to the bed.

Keep listening, he called to Kip. Keep listening for Angel to come.

The girl shut her eyes. Her hands twisted the blanket which Felix threw over her. Then she lay still. She looked crumpled and worn as an old pillow.

Felix thought of Angel. Dark and sinewed as bark. Tough and rooted as thistle. I've never heard her cry, he thought. The folds above his eyes contracted. He bent over and took one of the girl's hands between his thick fingers. It was not until the girl had come battering at his peace that he'd wondered at all about the pain of a growing root.

The girl cried out again and clutched at his hand.

He sat on the edge of the bed. The girl lay still.

If he could only shed his flesh, moult and feather again, he might begin once more.

His eyelids dropped. His flesh melted. He rose from the bed on soft owl wings. And below he saw his old body crouched down like an ox by the manger.

He reached for his fiddle. Then he heard at a distance the chatter of wheels on the rutted road.

13

James's horse still brought him on. Night had shrunk into the long shadows of the trees, into the slender shadows of the grass, into the flitting shadow of birds. Light defined the world. It picked out the shattered rock, the bleached and pitted bone.

It would edge the empty bottle on Felicia's table, James thought. It would lie congealed in the unwashed plates. It would polish the yellow of Traff's head and count the streaked tears under Lilly's eyes.

It would shine in his own empty mangers. On Kip's face. On Greta's bleak reproach. On the loose stones William had piled on his mother's grave.

Daylight called on him to look. To say what he had done. Yet he could see, he told himself, only as far as his eyes looked. Only as far as the land lay flat before him. Only up to the earth-tethered clouds. He could, too, he knew, look into his own heart as he could look into the guts of a deer when he slit the white underbelly. He held memory like a knife in his hand. But he clasped it shut and rode on.

He could not think of what he'd done. He couldn't think of what he'd do. He would simply come back as he'd gone. He'd stand silent in their cry of hate. Whatever the world said, whatever the girl said, he'd find her. Out of his corruption life had leafed and he'd stepped on it carelessly as a man steps on spring shoots.

The horse had brought him out on the brow of the hill. Below him he could see the road which ran up the creek past Felix Prosper's, past Theophil's, past the Widow Wagner's, past William's, round by the flat lake to his own gate. From the height of the hill the land below seemed ordered and regular, but as the horse slipped down over the shale into a clump of pines he wondered where in all the folds and creases he would find the girl. He remembered her words: What do you want me to do now? His silence. Greta's eyes behind him. Must the whole world suffer because Greta had been wronged? Must the creek dry up forever and the hills be pegged like tanned skin to the rack of their own bones?

Below in the valley he heard the creak of a wagon-box and the rattle of wheels. He wondered why he'd seen nothing on the road when he'd looked down from above. Theophil must be up and about some business of his own.

14

Theophil did not hear the wagon as it passed. He turned and pulled sleep about him like an empty sack.

15

It was Ara who drove the horses. Angel was beside her on the seat. The Widow sat on a heap of quilts and a feather bolster in the box. At each jolt of the wagon she called on God.

Angel looked over her shoulder.

He's given you lambswool and goose feathers, she said. What more do you want?

The Widow groaned.

Touch them up, Angel said to Ara as she looked at the team. Felix can't do anything but fiddle. The wonder is he stayed about at all.

Angel took the whip out of the socket. Ara's hands tightened on the reins.

What if they bolt? she said.

Dear God, the Widow said, shall I be drawn to death by my own son's team?

Loose the lines, Angel said to Ara, or they'll snap. You can't urge and hold a thing at the same time.

The horses broke into a trot. They tossed their manes and lifted their feet.

I never thought I'd be driving a team down this length of road, Ara said. Wherever I go I most often go by my own strength.

16

At the other end of the valley William and the boy still waited.

It seems a strange sort of thing, William said, to light another fire on the top of what fire has destroyed. The curious thing about fire, he said, is you need it and you fear it at once.

Every time a shoe has to be shaped, or the curve of a bit altered, or a belly filled, someone lights a fire. In winter we cry out for the sun, but half the time it's too hot, the butter melts, the cream sours, the earth crumbles and rises in dust.

With a stick he pushed away the embers from the foolhen which the boy had snared in the kinnikinic bushes.

The boy was sitting silent and restless beside him.

I did wrong to stop with you, the boy said. A grown man doesn't need someone to sit up with him no matter what the occasion.

A man needs living things about him, William said. To remind him he's not a stone or a stick. That he's not just a lone bull who can put down his head and paw the bank and charge at anything that takes his fancy.

He had taken the bird out of the ashes and was dividing the carcass.

You didn't stop, though, to stay with me, he said. You stayed because waiting is better than thrashing around. You stayed because if James comes you can settle your mind about what you really don't know.

I've been thinking, the boy said, that I didn't ride down past Theophil's. No one, he said, has asked Felix Prosper. Though what help one could get from Felix I don't know, he said, since Felix sits there like the round world all centred in on himself.

He drinks coffee like the rest of us, William said. Though, he said, I'd be hard pressed to know how he comes by the money to pay for it. If you think of it, he said, this case of Felix is a standing lesson for someone to think twice. A man who drinks coffee is dependent on something outside himself. But I myself doubt that he'd be much help to a person in trouble. He has troubles of his own if he cared to pick them up, but he lets them lie on another man's doorstep. He spends all his days lying round like a dog in a strip of sunlight taking warmth where he finds it.

I never heard of a dog brewing himself a pot of coffee, the boy said. The thing about a dog lying in the sunlight is it just lies in the sunlight. Perhaps no living man can do just that.

The two men sat in silence for a while watching the sun rise over the backs of the hills.

It's going to be another scorcher, William said, but the boy wasn't listening to him. He had heard a grouse rise on the hillside and boom down into a gully. Then he saw a horse and rider parting the branches on the lower slope. It was James. As he rode closer, the boy noticed that he was wearing a new plaid shirt.

William stood up.

He's been to town, the boy said. Perhaps he took Lenchen with him.

17

As Ara turned the team into the gate, she raised her head. The Widow sat upright on the lambswool quilts, her hands on the edge of the box. Above the chatter of a chipmunk which balanced on a bush near the cabin window, they heard a thin wailing.

Dear God, said the Widow, it's a feeble cry. Quick. Quick, she called and clambered down from the box as Ara pulled the horses to a stop before the door.

We don't want any trouble, Angel said as she jumped down from the seat.

The Widow's hand was on the knob.

If there's trouble, Mrs. Prosper, she said, it won't be of my making. Dear God, she said, the latch needs oil.

18

When James pulled his horse up at the foot of the slope he could see the gate, the stable, the path which led down from the stable-yard to the creek. Where the house had been there was nothing but blank smouldering space. On the fringe of the space he saw the figures of William and the boy beckoning to him.

In the emptiness of the fenced plot the bodies of the man and the boy seemed to occupy space which, too, should have been empty. The lank body of William and the thin body of the boy roped him to the present. He shut his eyes. In his mind now he could see only the seared and smouldering earth, the bare hot cinder of a still unpeopled world. He felt as he stood with his eyes closed on the destruction of what his heart had wished destroyed that by some generous gesture he had been turned once more into the first pasture of things.

I will build the new house further down the creek, he thought. All on one floor.

The men had come towards him. William's hand was on his sleeve.

We were waiting for you, William said. It was nobody's fault. I've seen it happen time and again. It's the women left, the meals that will never be ate, it's the heat and the frost and the empty spaces.

Tell him straight out, the boy said, that Greta burned the house and no one knows where Lenchen is. Make him speak.

Lenchen, James said. He looked at the burnt ground.

I left her here, he said.

And Greta, the boy said. It was her face we saw behind the honey-suckle. Where have you been that you left the two of them alone at such a time, and come back two nights and a day later dressed up in a new shirt.

James dug his toe into the edge of the ash, but he said nothing.

What made Greta set fire to things? William asked.

James looked up at him.

God knows, he said, we both had reason to wish the place gone and everything in it.

James turned to the boy. What could he say of the light that had made him want to drink fire into his darkness. Of the child got between the leafless trees when the frost was stiff in the branches. Of beating up Kip and running off because Kip had been playing round with the glory of the world.

I ran away, he said, but I circled and ended here the way a man does when he's lost.

I've a notion, William said, that a person only escapes in circles no matter how far the rope spins.

There was Greta as well as James, the boy said.

James turned away leading his horse as he went.

We best go down the creek, William said, and then we can think what to do. Ara'll make you welcome, he said to James, as long as you care to stop.

I wouldn't speak for Ma, the boy said.

He turned to James.

Tell me, he said, what would a girl do?

19

By Felix Prosper's stove the Widow sat with James's child across her knee.

Felix didn't do bad for a man, Angel said. Especially for a man who never raised a hand to help one of his own mares in foal. I doubt whether he ever knew the difference between what just happened and what other people did.

Hush, the Widow said. It's no time for remembering. Remembering churns grief to anger.

She laid her hand on the baby's back.

Dear God, she said, what a straight back he has.

He'll need it, Angel said, to carry round what the world will load on his shoulders.

20

Felix stood at the edge of his own brown pool. Kip sat on the bank beside him.

When a house is full of women, Kip said, and one of them Angel, it's best for a man to take his rest among the willows.

When a house is full of women and children, Felix said, a man has to get something for their mouths.

I've seen a bird, Kip said, wear itself thin doing just that. A bird with a whole nestful of beaks open and asking.

Felix played his line.

I keep thinking about James, Kip said. I kept at him like a dog till he beat around the way a porcupine beats with his tail.

Felix moved down the creek a little.

James's got more than a porcupine has to answer for, he said. How're you going to pick up a living now?

There's no telling at all, Kip said. There's no way of telling what will walk into a man's hand.

21

Ara was sitting at the foot of Felix's bed. The girl lay quite still, her yellow hair matted with sweat. From the next room came the sound of the Widow's voice and the sound of Angel's hand upon the stove.

Suddenly the girl sat up.

The door's opening, she said. I see James in his plaid shirt. He's lifting the baby in his two hands.

Ara stood up. The girl wasn't speaking to her any longer; she was speaking to James.

His name is Felix, she said.

Ara didn't want to look at James. She went to the window and leaned out across the bush where the sparrow chattered. Above her the sky stretched like a tent pegged to the broken rock. And from a cleft of the rock she heard the voice of Coyote crying down through the boulders:

I have set his feet on soft ground;
I have set his feet on the sloping shoulders
of the world.